BLACK SHEEP

K E Stokes

First published in 2025 by Blossom Spring Publishing
Black Sheep Copyright © 2025 K E Stokes
ISBN 978-1-917938-24-2
E: admin@blossomspringpublishing.com
W: www.blossomspringpublishing.com

Chapter 1

It had been the best day, and Gem was tickled pink with her new dress and all, swinging the department store carrier bag in the air as she skipped down the pathway. With the front door barely open, she shimmied past her mother's legs towards her bedroom.

"You go steady now – I'll be through in a jiffy," Hattie said.

Gem was in pants and vest, jogging on the spot as she waited for her mother to remove the tags.

"Arms up," Hattie said, placing the dress over Gem's head.

They both stood in front of the wardrobe mirror, admiring the reflection.

"Well, that's just perfect, look at you," Hattie said, as proud as punch.

"Thank you, Mummy," Gem said.

*

The kitchen resembled a bakery, covered in pastry and flour, with the window wide open to appease the stuffy heat of a hot oven. Hattie had made a cherry cake, and Gem was hovering in the background, waiting to lick away the dregs from the mixing bowl. As she carried it into the living room, Malc was sat in the armchair, peering over his newspaper.

"Mind your hands on the furniture," he said.

Gem laughed out loud and held out a sticky finger. "Do you want some?"

"No, I don't," he sneered.

"Neh, Lola likes it," she said.

The man seemed intensely agitated by Gem's continuous chatter, answering Lola's countless imaginary questions, so he grabbed the remote to crank up the telly volume.

"I can't hear," he said, like a right old mardy arse.

Hattie was looking on and then marched over to switch the channel to Gem's favourite TV show, *The Bear's Bones*. "There you go," she said, smiling.

It was maybe a little rude to deny Malc's existence and use the situation to administer a crafty marital poke, but he was having none of it and just stood from his chair, slung the newspaper under his arm and left the house.

"Daddy," Gem said, diving to the window.

"Leave him be," Hattie said.

*

The pram was unfolded and ready for Gem to climb in.

"Come on you, let's pop out before it rains," Hattie said, putting on her coat.

The daily fresh air ritual was a single lap around the block via Shoal Woods before calling at the village shop for sweeties on the way home. The shopkeeper had a habit of rabbiting on about any old shit, and Hattie wasn't good at halting the conversation, and so she waited for the next customer to reach the counter before leaving. Dark clouds eventually descended, and Hattie slung the rain hood over Gem, quickening her step through the ensuing puddles.

"Why do we always go for a walk?" Gem said.

"Because exercise is good for you, and Mummy needs to lose a little weight," Hattie said, patting her belly.

*

Gem loved to play in the back garden, feeding playdough-constructed biscuits to circle of cuddly toys. Hattie was hanging out the laundry when the phone rang, so she dropped the pegs and went inside to answer the call. She finally came back out, full of spit and bluster – and in the mind of a child there was no clear comprehension as to why.

"You okay, Mummy?" she said.

Hattie didn't answer and remained silent for the rest of the day. Gem started throwing her toys around and screeching like a banshee to get her mother's attention, to no avail.

*

The dullness descended into early evening, and Gem was expecting the usual bedtime routine where she and her mother would sit together on the sofa, drinking cocoa with Lola between them. Instead, all the lights were off and Gem was alone, standing on the rug in the middle of the living room, wondering what she had done wrong.

*

The clanging of pots stirred Gem from her bed, so she grabbed Lola and walked into the kitchen where her mother was by the sink, being purposely noisy. She pulled out a chair to sit at the table, and Hattie turned towards her with an evil and fixated glare.

"Who are you?" she said.

"I'm Gem, Mummy,"

"Yes, but *who are you*?"

"Stop it," Gem said, holding her hands up to her face.

Hattie stood over the girl in defiance, and then punched her square in the face – over and over again. The force knocked Gem to the floor, so she clambered back up, walked towards the back door and across the lawn to find shelter in the garden shed. With blood dripping from her face, she peered through the cracked and grimy window and saw Hattie on the back step, heaving and grunting like some raging statue.

*

At first light, an unbearable hunger drove Gem back to the house. The door had been left slightly ajar, and it felt eerily cold and unwelcoming. All signs of her very existence had been stripped away, including Lola, who she had left behind in a hasty retreat from her mother's fists. Personal mementos and framed snapshots had been cleared from the lounge dresser and fire mantle, as if to erase all connective memories.

Gem opened the fridge to find just enough milk to soak a small mound of cereal, which she devoured in seconds, wishing there was more. Some odious 'being', who bore no resemblance to her mother, thundered into the kitchen and continued on as if Gem weren't even there, humming some innocuous tune. The incomprehensible ignorance was purposeful, such that Gem's heart sunk once again into a hollow, meaningless space.

Chapter 2

Life beneath the shroud of Hattie's vile and uncompromising demeanour and batshit-crazy adaptations to the house were unbearable. Curtains remained closed, locks on every door – except the bathroom, of course – to remove Gem's fundamental right to privacy. A miserly and cruel mealtime regime left just enough food to prevent starvation as Gem fed on her mother's leftovers: a gnarled chicken bone, the remnants of whatever vegetable, and a dab of gravy. School lunchtime was equally precarious: Hattie refused to provide the funds, so Gem was expected to sit with her fellow pupils in the dining room, like a visitor among feasting monkeys at the local zoo. It was a compromising situation as there was no proviso for those whose parents who either couldn't or wouldn't pay their way. The deputy head had repeatedly challenged Hattie's claim that she was a welfare case, despite all opposing circumstances.

*

The bitterness of Malc and Hattie's failing marriage had fractured paternal ties, but despite her father's infrequent visits, Gem was always drawn to his side like an old dog whenever he graced the house. The physical and mental deterioration of a once joyous little girl waved many a red flag, much to Malc's denial that Hattie may be the perpetrator, so as not to 'shake the tree'.

Playing happy families in the Alhart household wasn't for the faint-hearted, as Mummy and Daddy hunched together 'elbow to elbow' at the tiniest of tables while Gem cooked for the cavalry. The underlying hatred stole the chance of any positive interaction that would invariably lead to another meaningless argument. The only consolation was that it gave Gem the luxury of an evening meal as opposed to bin scraps.

From the last glutinous mouthful, Hattie's hostility reigned, as she slumped on the sofa to watch some trashy soap for the brain-dead. It was as before on Dysfunction Alley: no convo, just 'schtum'.

"Would anyone like tea and biscuits?" Gem said.

"Yea, bring a plateful," Hattie said.

Gem's meagre attempt to reconcile the non-gathering served to simply halt Malc's departure. She watched as he stared blindly across the room, looking bored as fuck and picking at a loose thread on the chair's arm. It was the stupidest idea, as he didn't eat sugary things, and she would have probably stood more of a chance if there had been a whisky bottle on the tray.

"That's me done, lots to do," he said.

"Useless grotbag," Hattie said.

*

Mental fatigue often plagued Gem's concentration in the classroom, and she found herself leaning forward and then jumping backwards as the devilish boy who was sat directly behind kicked the underside of her chair.

"Will you stop that," she said, sneering at his stupid face.

"Weirdo," he said.

Physical education was Gem's favourite subject at school, but without a proper kit to speak of, she was consigned to the lost property box where the garments found were often too big and baggy for her bony frame. If only her mother gave the tiniest shit about adhering to school curriculum and provide her with the appropriate clothing.

She and Ava walked into the hall, its echoes accentuating the noise level and the sound of every cruel taunt from other pupils: "Neh, look at 'Spider-Legs'!", "Bone Yard!", "Greenfly!" and more.

"Someone been kicking the shit out of you, skinny-ass," Dev said, with a mouth like a trapdoor.

Gem had forgotten about Hattie's last 'booting across the floor' icky fit, which had produced several dark purple marks on her thighs.

"Just ignore them, idiots," Ava said.

The bell finally rang out and Mrs Piper called Gem over for the usual 'safeguarding' ritual to which her response was always the same: "Yes, yes, I'm fine – can I go now?" she mumbled, ever fearful of being late home. Such an inverted reaction conveyed much more than Gem realised, as did the many bruises that had been duly reported by the activity teacher. The ugly marks were beyond superficial and more ingrained and intense, suggestive of repeated angry blows.

*

The following morning, Gem was called to the main

office for more tick-box questioning: Was she happy with lessons? Did she want to discuss any problems or need any extra-curricular assistance? And so on.

"Did you fall and hurt yourself, pet?" Mrs Goldsmith asked, pointing to Gem's right leg.

"I slipped on some ice," Gem said, pulling down her flimsy, ill-fitting skirt.

"Really – I didn't think it had been that cold," Mrs Goldsmith said, scribbling some notes in a leather-bound notebook.

It wasn't the first time and it sure as hell wouldn't be the last. Maybe Gem should start wearing trousers, even in the summer, to hide any subsequent injury from prying eyes. Each report was always noted as per the authority requirements and then pushed aside time and again, as if that would somehow set it straight. It clearly didn't matter that it was a permanent problem and they needed to challenge repercussions regardless of immediate evidence.

*

Gem walked through the school gates where Dev and the gang were waiting. She continued, hoping they would just leave her be, but once she was far enough away, they herded her down a side street and gathered around the fresh meat. Dev stepped forward, to within an inch from her face.

"So, what's the deal with you, skank?" he said.

"I dunno, I could ask you the same question," Gem said.

When bullies descend it's probably best just to nod

and bow in all the right places, except Gem's feistiness took over, much to her own detriment. Dev slung her head back against the wall and kicked her shins with his stomper boots, while the other lads laughed at the resulting pain.

"You a girl anyways, let's have a look," he said, trying to rag up her shirt.

"Don't you dare," Gem said, kneeing the scumbag in the nuts.

As Dev buckled, his entourage didn't know whether to help him or thump her, and, at that point, she ran out from between them as fast as her crippled legs would go.

Gem took a different route home, through the woods where the air was sultry-warm, filled with ambient birdsong filtering through the trees. The unlikely escape roused a bitter lament, and tears fell from her eyes, stemmed anger raging from dry lungs. She just wasn't ready to return to school and so spent day after day in the woods, until the truancy triggered another safeguarding investigation, this time requiring a routine house call.

Mother was on the patio, slugging whisky and rye like a park-bench 'wino' when a care worker from social services pulled up outside the front gate.

"Could we have a word Mrs Alhart? It won't take long," a lady said, carrying a folder in one hand and a bag over the other arm.

"Of course, go on inside – can I make you a cup of tea or coffee, Mrs …?" Hattie craftily tipped the contents of her glass into the window basket before entering the house.

"No, I'm good. And please, call me Susan," she replied, alluding to the ID badge hanging on a ribbon around her neck.

*

The atmosphere was as sour as a barrel of lemons as Hattie tried to avoid the obvious, insisting that Gem was only cleaning the oven because *she* had a back injury and couldn't possibly kneel on a hard floor. The woman had clearly forgotten that, prior to Susan's arrival she had been joyously swinging her tits off on the garden seat out front.

"Surely, it could have waited until you were better?" Susan said.

"Well, maybe, but there'd been a spillage, and ..." Hattie said, teeming with fake excuses.

Susan beckoned Gem to the sofa. "Mrs Alhart, I am here because there have been some concerns about Gem not attending school – have you any idea why?" she asked.

Gem was on a knife-edge, pre-empting the aftermath like the sting of a thousand bees on bare flesh.

"No, but I am sure it won't happen again," she said.

"Can you explain the bruises on Gem's legs?" Susan said.

"It's the boys at school," Gem said.

"She's clumsy anyway, always walking into things. Could do with an eye test – what do you think, sweetie?" Hattie said.

"Well, I'm sure we can sort something out with the school optician – would that be okay with you, Gem?" Susan said.

10

"Suppose," Gem said.

Honesty had taken a nosedive – Gem could see perfectly well but went along with the bullshit pretence to appease her stupid mother. She didn't need another excuse to further draw attention, and there was no doubt that wearing glasses would feed an already raging beast.

Susan stood from the sofa and adjusted her handbag. "I'll see myself out," she said. Gem watched with intent, wishing she could follow her outside and spill her guts about what was really going on. Another failed opportunity passed without incident, leaving Hattie to continue spouting blatant lies to distract the authorities. Meanwhile, Gem's case would just shrivel to the merest fragment, placed among a forgotten pile of papers.

*

The false smiles and meek hospitality soon faded behind the ever-present, apron-clad monster. Revenge was a priority, but even Hattie could figure that inflicting further wounds would incite another meeting, so she did the next worst thing and launched Gem down the cellar steps. It was a torturous exercise to which she had grown accustomed, hours spent in a dark and solitary place, propped against a stone wall with her knees beneath her chin to battle the cold. The demoralising escapade of a woman whose sole compulsion was to pick Gem apart drew bitter tears.

It was hard to tell morning from night as there were no visible air vents in the cellar. The only sign was the turning key, finally releasing Gem from the insipid depths below stairs, sleepless and chilled to the bone, to prepare her mother's breakfast.

Gem's sister – or 'the privileged one' – was in the kitchen, screaming and wailing while Gem shuffled around like a walking corpse, wondering what the hell she had to complain about.

"Where've you been? You look like shit," Fran said.

"Why, thanks, sis, love you too," Gem said, giving her the finger.

It was never certain whether Fran was coming or going, as she and Gem rarely shared the same space. Another 'being' whose infrequent stop-offs showed nil regard for those who shared the same roof.

*

Hattie was busy stuffing her face with toast and eggs when a taxi rolled up outside the house, toot-tooting the horn. Fran eventually appeared from her bedroom, hauling several bags and a suitcase.

"See y'all whenever," she said, slamming an envelope down on the kitchen table. Whatever its contents, it quickly made its way into Hattie's apron pocket before she'd even wiped the breakfast remnants from her mouth with the edge of the tablecloth.

"Where's she off to?" Gem said.

"No idea, but she'll be back, you'll see," Hattie said.

What a privilege to live solely to please oneself, a flighty and ambitious passing ship with no ties or questions asked.

*

It was the end of another school day, and Gem was walking with Ava to the bus stop. The friendship was a treasured interlude, filled with much-needed laughter and tomfoolery, and as they were larking around Gem gave chase down the windy cobbled street.

"Come on," she yelled out.

Ava wasn't quite so sprightly and tripped on her shoelace, grazing her knee on the hard stone.

"Damn it, I'm so clumsy," Ava said.

"Come back to mine – we'll soon fix that," Gem said, helping Ava to her feet.

Following the 'off-the-cuff' suggestion, Gem hadn't really considered the implications of Ava entering the lion's den. She made up some story about her mother's regular afternoon nap and to be quiet when entering the house, but while cleaning Ava's wound with cotton wool and warm water, Hattie drifted into the kitchen.

"That looks nasty. Did you fall or were you pushed?" she said, spitting like an old cat.

"Oh, hello, Mrs Alhart – its fine now, thank you,'" Ava said.

"Would you like to stay for tea?" Hattie said.

"If it's not too much trouble," she said, having missed her bus and knowing it was at least an hour before the next one.

The random invite was beyond the realm of the woman's dubious nature and made Gem's teeth itch, a tad suspicious of some ulterior motive.

"Would you like to ring your grandma – she might be

wondering where you are?" Gem said.

"No, it's okay – she's got that thing where you can't remember stuff, so she wouldn't get it anyway," Ava said.

*

The girls were busy playing in the lounge when Hattie shouted them through to the dinner table that was royally furnished with a selection of sandwiches and a three-tier cake stand in the centre, stacked with sticky buns. A lemonade-filled fluted jug and accompanying glass tumblers were a classy addition to a seldom tea party, implying that such events were commonplace. Hattie had already apportioned some food on each plate, insisting that Ava take a seat nearer the kitchen window. The odd request went by the wayside, lost to Gem's insane hunger, drawing her like a magnet to the unlikely banquet.

"Your mum is nice," Ava said, chowing down.

"Do you think?" Gem said, with an inverted sarcasm.

"You should come with us to the country fair this weekend," Ava said.

"We'll see," Gem said.

Ava was a textbook case who lived with doting parents in a cosy little cottage on the outskirts of Lanebridge. Gem couldn't deny feeling a tinge of envy, wishing *she* was the one bound by no constraints and psychological affliction. She often wondered if other kids made assumptions of each other, and what would they make of her ravaged state, draped in raggy old-lady clothes and hair that had never seen a pair of scissors. All she ever wanted was to be normal, and therefore accepted.

*

The sound of furniture scraping across the floor echoed through the walls. Gem crawled from her bed to peek into the lounge where Malc was staggering about in the lounge, tearing strips off Hattie and yelling whisky-fuelled insults and accusations. Strangely gratified by the man's verbal diarrhoea, Gem crouched down by the door to listen further, like a bully on the sidelines.

"I dunno w-what the f-fuck happened t-to you," he slurred.

"Well, *he* should be dead, d'ya hear me? Fucking dead!" Hattie screamed.

The raging altercation made no sense, and Hattie finally left the scene, leaving Malc to stew in alcohol oblivion. What was the actual point of such a hellish relationship and why were they still married – a contradiction in terms?

*

Ava didn't show up for school the following morning and Gem spoke with Mrs Pineshore, who said that Ava had been puking through the night. The surprise feast immediately came to mind, along with Hattie's allocated seating arrangement, making it most likely intentional – and, therefore, fucking evil.

"Christ," Gem said, the colour draining from her face.

"I am sure she will be okay. There is a tummy bug going about," Mrs Pineshore said.

If only the teacher knew what Hattie was capable of and that she might have gone all out to harm an innocent child.

*

There had been no feedback from social services, nor any mention of Gem seeing the school optician following the home visit – unless, of course, Hattie knew otherwise. Influential whispers may have filtered through the walls of the old town hall where she once worked as a councillor, calling on some back-handed favour to gag the do-gooders. Even in the early days the woman was shifty and manipulative, especially among men who would sell their souls for a hand job.

*

Gem was relieved to see Ava back in the classroom, though she seemed a little different to previously. At the end of the final lesson, Ava quickly gathered her books and headed for the door as if her pants were alight.

"Wait for me! What's the rush?" Gem said.

"I have to get back, sorry," Ava replied, in full stride down the corridor towards the main entrance. She was clearly, though unconvincingly, lying through her teeth.

"Can't we just walk together?" Gem said.

"My auntie picks me up from school now."

"What about your grandma?"

It was all beginning to make perfect sense, as per Hattie's manipulative plan. Destroying the relationship had been intentional, so that Gem could spend more time tending to her mother's needs without distractions like friends and 'growing up', God forbid. It had also planted a twitchy little seed in her head to be wary of any future liaisons, should they suffer the same fate without reproach.

Chapter 3

Gem left school with no qualifications, ambition or sense of self, violated by a woman who saw her as an open wound over which to pour salt. She was broken, demoralised and void of trust, as was the foundation of a damaged individual. Thoughts of leaving home had crossed her mind many times, but with no money and little knowledge of life beyond the front door, freedom could only ever be a daunting prospect.

Each day mirrored the one before and began with the preparation of her mother's breakfast – muesli followed by a round of toast with two eggs and a large mug of gorilla-strength coffee to swill it down. Gem was then expected to hover around the table to clear away dirty pots while trying not to hear the sound of her mother clacking and slavering like a pig at a trough. Dinner was much the same, unless mother was out with the 'Cross Dollies' at the village café, and during such times Gem would inevitably miss out on lunchtime scraps. The woman's ever-increasing waistline evoked a constant dread of one day having to soap her copious flesh with a wet flannel and hoist her to a nearby piss pot.

Even though the house was aesthetically worn, with peeling paint and scuffed wallpaper, Hattie insisted the place was wiped down and swept daily, lest lingering spider webs inflame her arachnophobia. Gem was dusting down the main window bay and caught a glimpse of the paper windmill in the neighbour's garden through a gap where the curtains didn't quite meet.

"Get your nose out of there," Hattie said, banging her fist on the wall.

The thump startled Gem and, as she edged back, she accidentally knocked Lily – a beloved china doll – onto the floor, where it smashed into a trillion pieces. Just as the stinkiest shit was about to hit the fan, Fran flounced in through the front door and miraculously diffused the hostility. The imitation queen feigned an air kiss on Hattie's cheek, false eyelashes flickering to accentuate the exaggerated gesture.

"It's so nice to see again, my lovely," Hattie said.

"Hey, guess who's moving to the London office?" Fran said. "And why is Lily in bits on the carpet?"

"Don't you worry about that," Hattie said, flapping her hand as if to swat an invisible fly. At least it wasn't the insidious 'Daisy' – a piece of porcelain ugliness that had reigned over the mantelpiece for years.

Following the usual shallow chit-chat over tea and broken biscuits, Fran crept out of the lounge and down the hallway while Hattie slept on the sofa. It was always *the* reason for an impromptu visit, but Gem was privy to Fran's purposeful delving through her mother's belongings as if they were her own. The sound of rustling echoed in the distance as she rooted through cupboards, drawers, and boxes filled with old documents and paraphernalia.

"You're looking in all the wrong places," Gem said, poking her head around the bedroom door.

"Shush," Fran said, pressing her finger against her Revlon lipstick. "The old bitch has ears like a shithouse rat,"

"Okay, have it your way."

Such misdemeanours were blindly ignored anyway, just as Hattie disregarded countless visits from the constabulary during Fran's teenage years. It was to hell with the golden girl's longstanding criminality, subsequent embarrassment, and the personal loss it caused.

*

Another tedious trip the supermarket was pending and Gem slipped on her tired shoes that nipped at the heels and set out along the grassy pathway towards the main road. Hattie's shopping list was clipped to an envelope holding the exact amount of money, with no allowance made for occasional error or price variation. Mrs Oddly strapped her grandchild into the back seat of a red four-door coupé, while her daughter loaded the pram into the boot.

"Hello, dear," she said, peering over the car's roof.

Gem didn't really speak to the neighbours and struggled to raise an eyebrow in acknowledgement. When living in a world void of sentiment, happy events are just another meaningless irritation.

Shoppers littered the aisles of the supermarket, huddled together like penguins on an icecap. Tongues had been wagging for months, spreading hurtful rumours throughout the village that Gem had some sort of mental disability. Anyone who was considered 'below par' didn't fare well with the locals, as though they harboured a strange disease. Gem was a prime target, her hair like partly drawn curtains and skin as pale as chalk dust.

A young shop assistant kept looking over as Gem dithered over pennies, repeatedly removing and replacing items from the shelves. Whether it was genuine concern for the poor girl or the shallow empathy one feels for a stray dog, at least she was interested.

"My name is Simone. Can I help?" she said.

"It's okay – I just have to check the prices," Gem said, feeling a little foolish.

"Let's work through your list and you can pay with what you have. How does that sound?" Simone said.

"That would be great, thank you," Gem said, humbled by the girl's good nature.

The sun was blazing hot as Gem shuffled home with barely enough strength to lift her feet from the floor. The handles of Hattie's old shopping bags were straining her wrists and as she crossed the street, she tripped over and landed on the groceries.

"Oh, fuck – the eggs," she said, peering into the one bag where everything was coated in yellow slime. Her mother's reaction would be monumental. Knowing all of Hattie's likely triggers, clumsiness was tops.

Furniture and large wooden crates littered next door's garden, and Gem stood, her mouth gaping at the sight of the tall, dark-haired boy unloading boxes from the removal truck that was parked outside. She wasn't even aware that the house had been up for sale, such was the unearthly restriction of perpetually closed curtains.

"Hey, I'm Dan," he said, holding out his hand.

"Gem. Nice to meet you," she said.

Held by the gaze of those ocean-blue eyes, she lost her grip on the door key, which hit the ground and bounced beneath the rosebush.

"Let me help," he said.

"No, it's okay, really," Gem whispered, patting the ground furiously and wishing Dan would just dissipate into thin air. She was already in deep shit, with the cracked eggs, without being seen cavorting with the new boy in town.

The laborious trudge of her mother's footsteps churned Gem's cavernous stomach, as did the merciless reaction to life's incidental setbacks and consequential tantrums.

"I fell over, sorry," Gem said.

"Jesus, what the …" Hattie said, with a face full of disapproving creases. "Get the fuck out of my kitchen!"

"I could go back to fetch more eggs?"

"Go!"

*

Gem sat on her bed, head bowed and wishing she was a million miles away. Like the unpredictable lull between lightning and thunder, Hattie's revenge finally came with that unmistakable key turn, confining Gem to her room for the rest of the day without food or water. Thank God for the stash of discreetly stolen nibbles she kept hidden in a box beneath the bed: the odd cookie, a slice of stale bread, and random cereal flakes – anything was better than starvation.

While lightly dozing, Gem heard a gentle tap on the bedroom window. She climbed from her bed to part the curtains and met with those unmistakable dark-blue eyes glaring in, his voice barely coherent through the glass.

"What are you doing here?" she said.

"Are you in bed already?" Dan said.

"I was tired – you have to go," Gem said, shooing him away.

"Can I see you tomorrow?"

"No, now go."

Such a random and enticing invitation would have been the perfect scenario for most adolescent girls, but not for Gem, who was a prisoner – and a seriously plain Jane with a pitiful, shapeless figure and no tits. Only in her dreams was she free to be anyone, maybe a token cheerleader, walking hand in hand with her beau before surrendering her virginity beneath the pale moonlight. It didn't matter anyway, as Dan was fresh off the cart, his scent already making its way to the Lesky Girls – a herd of debauched females who seduced every male in Lanebridge.

Painful stomach cramps were growing ever stronger and increasingly distracting as Gem tried to focus on the pages of some old school library book to suppress the pain.

"Hey, I need the bathroom!" she said, thumping

repeatedly on her door until her fist ached.

After several agonising minutes, Hattie's incessant grumbling could be heard through the wood as she reluctantly turned the key.

To spare what was left of her dignity, Gem wedged an old chair beneath the bathroom door handle to undress privately. The water's laboured flow eventually filled the bath to a suitable level, and so she climbed in to soak her weary body beneath the warm, soapy surface. In the depths of her imagination, she was floating on the ripples of a secluded lake, the sun filtering through the cascading tree branches – a perfect scene, tinged by the drip-dripping of rusty taps. What price freedom, she thought, sensitised to her predicament and attuned to Hattie's prowls, like an animal's fighting instinct against predators.

Gem stood from the now tepid water and reached over for the single towel hanging over the handrail. She patted her skin with the pitiful mass of dangling threads and noticed a streak of bright red blood flowing down from between her legs.

"Oh no, not now," she said, her eyes pooling with tears at what was surely the start of her first menstrual period. The regular pubescent milestone was, in her world, quite literally a curse, and she was instantly fixated by 'what ifs' – how would she find sanitary protection and how could she withstand her mother's fury should she stain the bed sheets? To make matters worse, Hattie was already banging on the doorframe.

"What *are* you doing in there?" she said.

"Hold on, I'm nearly ready," Gem said, clumsily gathering her threadbare dressing gown around her waist with what was left of the tie-belt.

Hattie couldn't wait any longer and violently shoved her way into the bathroom, fracturing the chair into several pieces. She launched Gem across the hallway, where she fell into a crumpled heap like a startled hedgehog by the roadside.

There was a knock at the door, and Gem didn't want to be seen in such a state, so she limped out of sight and towards her bedroom. The house rarely had visitors and so Gem was doubly curious to see a woman on the step, holding a large ceramic dish flanked by a red chequered cloth. Hattie finally answered the call, clearly disgruntled by the intrusion.

"Hi, I'm Lily – I've baked an apple and blackberry pie for you and your daughter," she gushed.

She continued to ramble about being the new neighbour, that her son was handy with tools and could fix anything. Hattie was just staring at the cake and promptly snatched it away before slamming the door on the well-intentioned woman. "Welcome to my world," Gem said.

The blood was now a brown, crusty stain on the skin of Gem's inner thigh that she had tried to scrub away with spit and the edge-seam of her dressing gown. While Hattie was busy stuffing her face with fruit-filled pastry, Gem casually walked through the kitchen and took a pair of scissors from the drawer. She had found an old bed sheet in the wardrobe and proceeded to cut it into strips and then layer with sheets of toilet paper. Creating makeshift sanitary towels when the real thing was readily available in every supermarket was a sad yet resourceful attempt at dealing with a personal adolescent crisis.

*

The bin was a putrid and stinking mass, left to fester because Hattie refused to put the damn thing out beyond the garden gate for collection. Gem was trying to squeeze in one more bag of trash when she noticed a white envelope stuck to the inside. She peeled back the soggy flap and found an old letter that had been torn into several pieces. Despite the paper trauma, Ava's writing was still recognisable on what appeared to be a party invitation. Hattie's wanton destruction of their friendship was bad enough, without discovering that she had also missed the chance to reconcile what had been lost. Gem was so very hurt and angry, and – although slating the old witch would be tantamount to screaming down a mineshaft – she marched back into the house, clutching the discarded remnants.

"This was *my* letter, from Ava – the girl you tried to poison, remember?" she said.

The stinging words just fell out of Gem's mouth, and she feared another beating or night in the cellar as retribution, but Hattie didn't rise to the vile accusation.

*

Lifeline: an aptly named journal, kept between mattress and bedframe that Gem had created with paper sheets and bound together with clips and bits of string. This was her only platform on which to openly express her misery and despair, periodically filled with written entries and illustrations, often so deep and ingrained they left puncture marks in the paper. The depravity, abuse and neglect were featured topics, as was the destruction of anyone or anything that stood in the way of time spent slaving for her mother. What started as a once-only rant was now a continual barrage of spit and guts, set to continue – should there be enough pages.

*

The appropriate materials had been laid out on the kitchen table for Gem to clean the decking out front. There was considerable yardage to cover, and Gem's hands were already in tatters from repeatedly scrubbing with an old wooden brush, its bristles like spikes, cutting into her skin. Hattie was out for lunch with the 'Cross Dollies', giving Gem the chance to take a well-earned break, or at least that was the intention. She sat herself down on the garden swing and began rocking back and forth, oblivious to her mother sneaking back down the path. Suddenly the sun disappeared behind a growling shadow, its putrid stench of stale coffee churning her guts.

"Get off your lazy, godforsaken ass *now*!" Hattie yelled.

Mrs Oddly, busy trimming the privet, stopped briefly to listen, being a nosy old boot.

"Another lovely day isn't it, dear?" she said.

"Why don't you mind your own business?" Hattie yelled back.

Gem didn't dare stop again and continued on until every square inch was as clean as it was possible to replenish old wood. While packing away, a vintage Jag rolled up outside the garden gate, a rare sight in such a quiet and understated neighbourhood.

The lowly engine grunt caught Gem's attention, but she certainly wasn't expecting to see her father behind the leather-clad steering wheel.

"Come on, climb in," he said

"I can't – look at me," she said, covered in dirty water stains.

He was pristine in a brand-new suit, as opposed to his usual ragged attire that was thinning at the knees and elbows. Maybe he did have another woman, Gem mused – if only to gratify his sexual urges.

"Is this yours?" she said, running her hand along the car bonnet.

"No, it belongs to a friend and he owes me one, so get in."

"Okay, where we going?"

"You ask too many questions. Fasten the seatbelt, so I can be off before your mother shows," he said.

"She'll lose her shit when she finds me gone," Gem said.

He patted her thigh and promised to talk to her when they got back – like Hattie would ever listen to anything he had to say.

Malc continued on through Lanebridge village towards the motorway: an expanse of open lanes filled with cars hurtling at double speed and heading for places Gem never knew existed. The random thrust into unknown territory wasn't quite a euphoric thrill, and she felt a little queasy.

"Not long now," Malc said.

"That's good, 'cos it's so hot in here," Gem said.

*

The car park alone was twice the size of the supermarket and Gem couldn't believe the amount of traffic and people milling about. Malc opened the passenger door and held out his hand to help her out of quite a low seat. They walked together towards some sliding doors, which slid open to reveal a palatial hallway lined with elaborately framed paintings and ornate furniture. The culinary aromas stirred her hollow stomach in anticipation of a wholesome meal, as was the customary pleasure of a girl who ate solely to survive rather than for pleasure's sake.

"Why are we here?" she said.

"You'll see," he said, smiling.

There was just too much to take in: salubrious décor, fancy mirrors and a sparkling chandelier that hung directly above their table. Gem was the child in a toy shop, enveloped by everything all at once.

"Here you go, choose whatever you like," Malc said, handing her the restaurant's glossy, three-fold menu.

She turned it back to front and then upside town, lost

in pictures of elaborate dishes and endless descriptions thereof. A waitress drifted over, holding a tiny notepad and pen.

"What does *she* want?" Gem asked of her father, albeit with an innocent heart.

"*She* is here to take your order," Malc replied, pointing back to the menu.

The choice was mind-blowing, and having scanned the menu's contents ad nauseam, Gem finally settled on the house burger with fries, a side of onion rings and a strawberry milkshake. The waitress seemed bemused by such naivety and smirked at a nearby colleague as she left the table.

This delightful excursion evoked Gem's wishful thinking. This was, in fact, her life and not some miserable existence in *that house* with a one god awful mother. Malc reached into the inside pocket of his jacket and pulled out a large pink envelope.

"This is for you," he said.

At that very moment, the wait staff gathered round the table to present her with an iced chocolate cake and a vocal ensemble of 'Happy Birthday'. It was altogether strange, as Gem had never known any such celebratory tradition and that she was expected to blow out the sixteen flickering candles.

*

It had been the best afternoon, if a little marred by thoughts of Hattie's perpetual anger when she arrived home. Punishment for doing no wrong is just twisted logic, but acceptance makes it easier to live with: "I'm clumsy, thoughtless, irritating", etc., and therefore deserving. Gem hoped that one day Malc would stop being so damn selfish take some responsibility for her wellbeing. Maybe then she could try and forgive him for abandoning her in infancy and leaving a peasouper – a mysterious mental crock of confusion.

*

Hattie's po-face glared through the kitchen window as the Jag pulled up outside the house.

"Don't you worry, I'll take care of this," Malc said.

Gem followed him through the door and sat down on the sofa. Malc knew Hattie had scuttled off to her bedroom and that she knew he would go find her. There was a single slice of banana cake left on a plate in the middle of the lounge table, so she reached over to take a bite.

"What the—?" she said, spitting out a gritty blob of sour sponge.

There were no signs of agitation or raised voices, so Gem was a little bemused when Malc finally reappeared, all smug like some two-bit hero. It seemed all too easy, and he had more than likely been taken in by Hattie's play-acting.

"Don't go, not yet," Gem said.

"I have to be somewhere, pet," he said, already backing towards the door.

The rumble of the Jag's engine had barely faded when Hattie resurfaced to wield her spiteful vengeance and obliterate every ounce of pleasure derived from Gem's first ever birthday celebration.

"You don't leave this house unless I say so," she said, grabbing a fistful of Gem's jet-black hair with which to swiftly launch her into the dungeon below stairs.

Gem banged and kicked the door as it slammed tight shut.

"You are such a cow — I hate you!"

The cackle of Hattie's derisory laughter twisted the knife further, and Gem struggled to contain the rage burning within. She may as well be dead.

A flimsy cotton dress offered little insulation, and it was hard to keep a limb still, cocooned by the cellar's dank, stony walls. Gem could just make out the metal boxes that were stacked close by and a fusty old blanket that was draped over them. It was crusty and stank of stale paraffin, but it was better than the ravages of frosty air on bare skin. Solitary confinement can twist all sense of proportion, and the pain of her meaningless existence led her down a sinister path of self-destruction. Knowing where her mother kept a plethora of painkillers and leftover antibiotics made suicide a very real possibility and was strangely comforting. She could die, and her mother would simply bury her body in the garden and continue on as before. Malc would maybe ask where she was, in passing, and the old bitch would just cough up some story that Gem had run away. There was barely a connection to the outside world since Gem had left school – no job, no longstanding friends or other relatives, so no trail: girl erased.

*

Within a myriad of loose ends, Gem tried once again to piece together a particularly harrowing childhood memory of a violent argument between Malc and Hattie. She could remember running into her bedroom to escape her mother's inconsolable sobs and then Malc rifling through wardrobes and drawers, stuffing clothes into a suitcase. It was a terrifying scene for a child, but, despite her tears, he just thundered past and back down the stairs without saying a word. There was no marriage after that, just unfinished business and an inability to split from each other for whatever reason, i.e. selling property and dividing belongings, and divorce, all of which incurs considerable legal fees.

The feeling of emptiness and devastation stirred her guts and she threw up what felt like slimy remnants of banana cake all over the cellar floor. In a sort of pre-hypothermia, Gem fell into a deep sleep while propped against a cold stony surface, exhausted from shivering and shaking.

Finally, the gloom of a windowless hollow was broken with the clunk of the cellar door key. Gem slowly shimmied up the wall until she was upright, her feet like blocks of ice.

"Come on, I haven't got all day," Hattie said, waiting on the bottom step.

The climb towards the door felt like a million miles, behind her mother, who was going purposefully slow.

Gem finally crawled into bed like a dying bird, dithering beneath the covers until her body temperature thawed back to some kind of normal.

*

It was around midday when Gem awoke to the stench of her vomit-soaked dress. She looked down and saw an elaborate gift box with a large pink bow from her father, poking out from beneath the bed, that he must have somehow sneaked past Hattie's prying eyes. Gem stuffed it to the back of her wardrobe, else it be consigned to the trash, just like Ada's letter.

Gem had never been so hungry, so much so that she would eat anything to ease the borderline retching and constant swallowing. She stepped into the hallway onto a scattering of upturned drawing pins, stabbing and cutting her feet. It was so obviously Hattie and her petty revenge because Gem had dared to sleep through breakfast. At least there were roast chicken drumsticks in the fridge. They had probably been there for days, but it mattered not as Gem promptly tore into the white flesh and sinew, stripping the bones dry and wishing there were a dozen more.

The unexpected feast had brought light relief and a welcome change from leftover pie crust and fat slivers. Gem returned to her bedroom to open the elaborate gift box, and found, beneath the papery shreds, that it contained selection of ornate bottles filled with various potions and a silver heart necklace in a velvet pouch. She wanted to believe that it meant something, albeit a materialistic expression of love, and not just an obligatory gesture. Hattie's prophylactic drugs were hardly an uplifting crutch on which to lean, to imagine her days being so unbearable that death was an enticing proposition.

*

The mundane trip to the supermarket was Gem's once-weekly chance to breathe in clean air and allow the merest snippet of real life to pass her by. The shopping list had been slid beneath Gem's bedroom door and required a shopping trolley to house a plethora of extra items. While trawling the aisles, Simone showed up to offer her welcome assistance.

"I'll open a new till when you're done, and then help you carry the bags home. Deal?" she said, smiling.

Gem was humbled by the girl's overtly caring and considerate nature, like an angel without wings, though not entirely comfortable about jumping the queue. She felt sure there were nearby voices whispering and cussing, "That's the weirdo girl, pushing in." Any preferential treatment would only blot her copybook in the eyes of the villagers, and that would never do.

Simone helped to pack all the bags and left the supermarket to help Gem carry everything home.

"Won't you get into trouble?" Gem said.

"Nah, I'll just work through my lunch hour to make the time up. Why doesn't your mother come with you – is she unwell?" Simone said.

"Not really," Gem said.

It was a perfectly understandable question, and pretty soon Simone would be able to form her own judgment, having seen for herself what type of woman Hattie really was. They continued in silence, treading grassy pastures and saddled with groceries, most of which were probably incidental.

They reached the garden gate and Hattie immediately opened it. "Well, looky here," she said, her sanctimonious bulk dominating the scene.

"This is a lot of shopping for one girl to carry," Simone said, defying the woman's patronising tone.

It wasn't like Hattie to recoil, thwarted ever so slightly by Simone's feistiness.

"If you need anything, anything *at all*, you know where I am," Simone said, raising her perfectly tweezered eyebrows.

"Thank you!" Gem shouted, as Simone walked back down the path.

Hattie couldn't stay quiet for long. "Who was that?" she said, with ruffled feathers.

"Simone, an assistant at the supermarket who offered to help, as I only have one pair of hands," Gem said. "So be grateful, damn it."

The logic was indisputable, unless of course your goal was to feed off the consequential struggle.

Desperate times can often skew all logic, and Gem had fought with the idea of telling Simone about her mother's abusive nature, hoping it would be reported to social services. Hattie was on record for being unreasonable, and the inconclusive findings on Gem's school record could at least raise a little interest. It wasn't without risk and could result in Gem being taken into foster care until she was eighteen, thus placing her in a worse predicament – if such a thing were possible. A metaphorical arm-link with someone whose influence could prove beneficial was maybe clutching at straws, such was Gem's desperation.

*

The sight of Dan's posh-boy looks peering through her bedroom curtains stole Gem from a particularly important *lifeline* rant.

"You can't keep doing this," she said, whispering through the glass.

"Come to the woods with me, it'll be fun," Dan said, smiling.

It perhaps wasn't the best time to ask, with frustration and misery already at the tip of her pen, so to hell with shallow hesitation. She quickly clambered through the window and across the grass, walking in front of Dan to remain incognito until out of sight. It was natural for him to assume that something didn't quite add up, and why was she tethered like a captured bird on such a beautiful day?

"You really are … unique," Dan said.

"What do you mean?" Gem said.

"So, what's the deal with your mother?"

"I help her, that's all," Gem said, in her vague attempt to justify the unjustifiable.

"But you are always in your room?"

It wasn't always an accolade to be different, and in days of old she would have been dragged to the stockades for all to mock and throw stones.

The afternoon of unexpected freedom was exhilarating, as Gem and Dan circled the woodland, lost in conversations about nothing in particular. It was enough just to stroll the pathways without shopping bags dragging down her tired shoulders.

"You should go back to school, do some studying," he said.

"Mm," Gem said.

And to think it was that simple, that everyone had the luxury of making such choices. He was already in sixth form and looking forward to going to college and then on to university to study law – such was the archetypical traditional family mascot. His mother had probably already cleared a space on the mantel for his framed graduation snapshot. Such prestigious belief in one's offspring is self-affirming, hence Dan's confident demeanour and desire to succeed. At best, she could only imagine what it would be like to leave Lanebridge village to start a 'freshman' year, her mother's pride in her pocket.

Gem had left the window latch purposely loose to allow easy access back into her bedroom and, while steadying herself on the chair strategically placed beneath the sill, heard Hattie rumbling around outside the door. It was pure luck that Gem's absence had seemingly gone undetected, and despite gambling with the purposeful destruction of yet another blossoming friendship, she found the deceit strangely gratifying.

*

Aunt Rosie pulled up outside in her high-spec Mercedes: a gold coin among old pennies in such an ordinary suburban neighbourhood. The woman was the director of a successful furniture franchise and lived in a five-bedroomed house within acres of land somewhere up north. Despite family ties, it was her first trip to Lanebridge, making it all the more mysterious. Hattie had been busy preparing lunch for her arrival, which would explain the recent shopping hoard. Gem could only hope that Hattie had no intention of poisoning her sister for material gain.

"Come and get it," Hattie cooed from the kitchen.

The rose-tinted farce to impress Aunt Rosie was a little nauseating, but another random opportunity for Gem to eat a substantial meal instead of her mother's left-overs.

The small wooden table was spruced up with shiny cutlery and a vinyl-coated tablecloth, fresh from the kitchen drawer and still with visible folds. The siblings sat adjacent to each other – the fancy sister donning a designer trouser suit and an apron-clad Hattie with raggy hair and chipped fingernails. Gem was sat with a much more discernible view through the kitchen window.

"Gemima, it's nice to meet you," Rosie said. "How do you stay so slim?"

Gem cringed at the sound of that name but bit her

tongue so as not to ruin the pretentious family reunion.

"Tuck in," Hattie said, while stacking her own plate with half the buffet.

Rosie selected a lone sandwich, sneering as she parted the bread to check its contents.

"The place is looking a little dated. I could get a substantial discount on some new furniture – I have a brochure in the car," Rosie said.

"I'm fine, thanks," Hattie said.

The women played nice for a while, cackling on about the weather and incidental stuff. There was no denying the obvious hostility choking the room, as the ladies pretended to like each other. Gem took advantage of the precarious situation and stuffed her cardigan pockets with sausage rolls.

"You'll have to come and see the horses," Aunt Rosie said, pulling a silk handkerchief from her patent-leather Gucci bag.

"I'd like that," Gem said, half-smiling.

*

Gem went to her bedroom, leaving the sisters to shuffle and writhe in their seats as if they were grease-coated.

"You don't need the money," Hattie said.

"Well, *he* wants to divide it equally between us," Aunt Rosie replied.

The clinking of spoons punctuated the bitter ruse, and the contrived meeting soon drew to an awkward close. Aunt Rosie stood to announce her departure, scraping her chair backwards across the kitchen floor.

"I take it you won't be at the will reading?" Aunt Rosie said.

"You know I can't travel across two counties for that, for Christ's sake."

Discussions about family inheritance can be difficult, especially when there is avarice and greed on the table, and Hattie was hell-bent on swaying their late father's decision. There were no tears or remorse, just her incessant whining over what she considered to be an unsatisfactory share.

Gem had never met her grandfather, nor had any recollection of meeting any other relatives before Aunt Rosie. The question remained whether all connections had been purposely severed by Hattie, or vice versa, because she was so utterly vile. The teensiest taste of financial gain and Hattie was fluttering like a moth to a light bulb.

*

With Aunt Rosie gone, Hattie's transparent and overwhelming bitterness was a bubbling under, like a dormant volcano. She went all out to antagonise, insisting that Gem help clear the table and then proceeded to throw each pot and plate that she placed on the drainer back into the water. "Use the dish rag!" she screeched.

"No, *you* use the dish rag," Gem said.

"Don't you talk to your mother like that," Hattie said, clawing at Gem's back as she turned away.

"You are *not* a mother," Gem said.

*

There was a note pinned to Gem's bedroom window:

Let's go to the woods again –same time tomorrow?
Dan x

Torn between a longing to see some boy and an underlying fear of being discovered, thus sabotaging their liaison secrete, was a complication no adolescent girl should have to endure. And what of Dan's inevitable sexual advances? Gem didn't have the merest clue about sex, or how she should respond, or even if she wanted to. Previous schoolyard recollections of girls loitering in shady corners, their skirts hitched up while the lads fiddled with their dicks, didn't exactly sell it for pleasure's sake.

One lousy minute past seven and Hattie's fists were already thumping hard and fast on Gem's bedroom door, feigning the depths of starvation. She leapt out of bed, trying not to retaliate with some cheeky retort, while dressing in double-quick time.

Hattie was on monotonous replay, waving her arms in the air and barking orders between coffee gulps. She insisted Gem prepare an outfit for her to wear for lunch with the 'Cross Dollies': undergarments, stockings and all. The demands were becoming more and more intense, once again, filling Gem's head with darkened thoughts of an immobile mother who required a permanent carer until her eventual demise. She would rather hack off her arms with a blunt knife than be subjected to such misery.

*

And so, another sneaky meeting with Dan had been

arranged. It was now on the cards, as a justifiable reward for delving through Hattie's smalls. Gem made doubly sure her mother was *gone* before setting a foot on the path, aloft at the prospect of Dan's company. She could see him swaggering in the distance, carrying a large bag over his shoulder.

"Wait up," she yelled, quickening her step. "What you got there?"

"Just some nibbles and fresh apple juice – oh, and a piece of home-baked chocolate roll," he said.

With a perpetual and often debilitating desire to fill her belly, Gem's priority suddenly shifted to finding a suitable feasting spot. She watched with intent as Dan laid out the picnic blanket beneath a sprawling tree.

"Get what you want," he said.

"Thanks," Gem said, fighting the desire to scoff like an esurient beast.

Dan didn't care about the food, the weather or surroundings, and was more eager to announce his two-year social studies course at college, and his mum's recent recce to secure suitable accommodation. There would also be a bank account: a financial drip to cover all costs, including new clothes, the purchase of train tickets to and from home at term times, and whatever else one required to comfortably experience the student lifestyle. She of perpetual unhappiness was miffed by the boy's fortunate disposition, wondering if he was truly appreciative of such privilege.

"So, what's next for you?" he said.

"Oh, I dunno, not much," she said.

There was more pleasure to be had right there than in yakking on about unachievable goals.

"It's like you've not eaten for days," he said.

"Maybe I haven't," she said.

Gem dabbed her mouth with a paper napkin, pondering their strange collaboration – the boy with the world at his feet and a flightless bird, gazing up to the sky.

"Why don't you tie back your hair? You really shouldn't hide such a pretty face," he said, stroking her sallow porcelain skin.

The defining moment of pleasure and pain had finally arrived, his warm spearmint breath dancing on her skin, igniting an arousing pulse between her legs. This was new territory, as was the reciprocating boner pressing against her thigh. With their lips barely aligned, the desire to gratify what she had longed for was here for the taking. He laid her down, with arms like tentacles, pulling and tugging shirt buttons and zips – and then their bodies entwined, writhing and shifting the blanket beneath them. Gem felt a sharp stinging pain as he entered her, and within a few grunts and moans, it was all over.

The sweaty lovers sat up and reassembled clothing, occasionally glancing at each other to acknowledge what had just happened. Gem was no longer a virgin – pure and untouched, and also a little naïve – having had sex with no protection, something school sex education classes had warned every female about.

"Maybe you should have used a condom," Gem said.

"I know, sorry."

"Well, it's too late now," Gem said.

*

Thankfully Gem managed to arrive home minutes before her mother, who flounced in, giving several waving hand swirls to see off the 'Cross Dollies' before tossing her coat and handbag on the kitchen table. Everything seemed relatively normal until an unexpected turn on a sixpence, and Hattie's eyes scrunched up like slits in putty.

"I've seen you with that boy –sneaking around behind my back," she said, her fat fingers jabbing into Gem's chest.

"What boy?" Gem said, quaking in her ill-fitting shoes.

"That dickweed from next door, that's who – well, there'll be no more of that," she said, her chins wobbling. "What in God's name does he want with a skinny runt like you anyhow?"

It was just as Gem had predicted, but no less hurtful. The woman's evil intentions were growing ever tighter and more restrictive, and to further deepen the hole, Hattie took great pleasure in announcing that it was the boy's mother who blew the merry whistle on their blossoming relationship. So much for the fruit pie bullshit – she was just like all the other 'villagers': a deluded nose rubber whose nasty, belittling judgements divided Lanebridge society.

A deep and entrenched feeling of loneliness and bewilderment dug deep into the paper fibres of Gem's angst-filled journal, while her mother jabbered on the phone to some such, discussing various arrangements.

"You have a job, starting Monday morning," Hattie said, poking her head around the bedroom door. "And don't be fucking late."

"So who will look after your fat, lazy ass?" Gem whispered.

"What?"

"Where is it?"

"At the church – they want a cleaner."

There was no mention of money, for how many hours or on which days. Not that it mattered – she might as well slave somewhere else as do it at home. Her place was to sit, shit and stand in accordance with Hattie's ever-changing rulebook.

*

The church was a little further away than the grocery store, down some country lane that bordered Lanebridge Farm. Gem walked through the church grounds towards the large wooden entrance that was already gaping open.

"Hello – is there anyone here?" she said, stepping inside.

The door was heavy and closed behind her with a clunk that echoed through the vestibule. While waiting in the darkness, an elderly guy appeared from the shadows.

"Nice to meet ya, young 'un – I'm Mr Rake, the church warden," he said, offering a cold, bony hand.

The man was vagrant: grubby and stinking of piss, triggering Gem's sensitive gag reflex. He explained the terms, as negotiated with Hattie, and that she would work for four hours, three times a week, at a rate of ten pounds an hour. It would have been lucrative, but for Hattie's cut of at least half the wages earned.

"Come on now, I'll show you round," he said, leading Gem through the graveyard towards the vicar's house. Her job was to clean the living room, the kitchen, the vicar's study, and toilets both upstairs and down and was given keys to the main door and the cupboard where all the necessary products were kept. The place didn't seem dirty enough to warrant such a regular service, so at least it would be easy.

Mr Rake eventually left the room, which was just as well: the man wreaked like a rotting sewer. Gem set to work, gathering up her hair with a slide and tuned in the old radio that sat on the windowsill. There was a spider's web draped along the curtain's edge, dotted with flies and other crumpled insect remains, with its keeper resting beneath.

"Let's get you out of there," she said, searching the place for a suitable box or container. *She* wasn't like her mother, scared half to death by the tiny creatures with legs like cotton thread.

Gem was wiping and tickling the furniture with a long feather duster when she dared to think about Dan and their recent sexual interlude. She had expected to feel something more, a magnetic pull, a desire to do it over and again, but it was just an act – and a pretty short one at that. The learning was simple: all body parts were interactive, despite a lapse in common sense, and alas she had experienced a taste of womanhood.

The first shift was over and Gem left the church, saying goodbye to Mr Rake, a stifling presence who cared not for personal boundaries. She walked through the neglected grounds towards the black iron gate, passing gravestones skewed like crooked teeth and empty beer cans littering the pavement. The local winos probably used the place as a hangout after dark, seeing as it was open for all to enter. So much for having a caretaker, she thought.

*

Gem arrived home a little late, to find a knife and fork either side of an old, greasy placemat on the table – the subtlest reminder that work commitments were no excuse to evade dinner. But first she rinsed out an old jar to make a new home for 'Mr Legs', adding bits of old paper and cotton wool for him to hide within the layers. The desire to nourish the mini-beast was admittedly spiteful and driven by Hattie's fear of spiders, like a cross to a vampire.

Power is transferable, justified by our own reasoning.

*

The cleaning job had grown borderline intolerable, working for a stinking scrap of a man whose repugnance resembled the ghouls of one's darkest nightmares. The constant intrusions or "just popping in" on Gem to see if she needed anything were non-productive – and where was the vicar, for whom she had been cleaning, preening and polishing thrice weekly? There was no sign of domestic life: fresh paperwork on the desk, a used coffee cup, or shoes by the door, and the church wasn't even open to the public. Maybe Rake was just using him as an excuse to get some young girl in, and Gem could be one of several he had since suffocated with his stifling presence.

Friday's shift was a little longer than the other days, and Gem was sauntering aimlessly through the church grounds and down the rugged path towards home. Glancing ahead, she drew in a sharp breath at the sight of Dan walking down the street with one of the Lesky girls, smoking weed and groping her tits – and in public view, for God's sake.

"Hey, how's your mother?" he scoffed.

"Go fuck yourself – it'll certainly last longer," she said, crossing the road in double-quick time.

Such a heart-wrenching and disrespectful pose was a massive slap around the face, eroding her trust in one fell swoop. He was just a cad, a no-mark who just wanted to shag her bones and nothing more. So much for the sleazy small talk, as if butter wouldn't melt.

Once again, Gem detoured through Shoal Woods to clear her head, the only reliable distraction from the Hattie trials and their lingering echoes – she was living within an invisible cage, controlled and manipulated by her mother's continual outbursts: "You will, you won't, you can't, because I say so." In nature, birds fly, trees grow, and flowers spread their petals whenever, in accordance with no one. This place was the only reason to be alive, its offer of escape, at will, into the wilderness and away from *that house.*

*

It seemed a little weird to see Dan's mother in the garden, fake-preening the flowers – another punch in the throat after what had just happened. Judging by the grovelling smile, Gem sensed a little guilt and remorse from the backstabbing chunder-snake.

"How are you today?" She bowed.

"I was fine until I saw that grotbag son of yours on my way home,"

"You've changed your tune, my girl."

"I certainly have – must be something to do with that slag he was groping in the village, and smoking weed must be a college-boy thing. Not so gracious now, eh?"

The old girl was stunned, with mouth open and garden pincers aloft. Spitting dust and bullets wasn't usually Gem's way, but she had to hit back somehow. Retribution slakes a vengeful thirst, and that particular spat was undeniably quenching.

*

A long-awaited letter was lying on the doormat, drawing Hattie like a magnet to metal. With pinched lips, she carefully sliced the envelope open so as not rip what she assumed was the eagerly awaited bequest from her late father. Strange how the windfall had somehow restored her capability to suitably dress and walk to the village bank to make the deposit.

While the cat was off elsewhere, Gem prepared a boiled egg and scavenged what was left of her mother's breakfast plate. She was clearing the table when she heard the gate's catch rattle, closely followed by several loud thumps on the front door. Most people just knock, so whoever it was had every intention of being heard: yesterday. Mr Rake was on the step, shuffling back and forth and cussing about having to wait, and must have known that Hattie wasn't around to stir the shit pot. Gem reluctantly opened the door ever so slightly, coughing and spluttering to feign the lurgy.

"Hello, dearie, can I come in?" he said, cupping his bony hands together.

"Not really. I don't feel well," she said.

"But you also have a job to do," he said, forcing his way in and swathing her like a dirty cloak.

"I told you, I have a stinking cold," Gem said.

"You're lying, little 'un – you come here now," Lake said, back-shuffling her towards the wall.

"Get the fuck away from me!" Gem yelled. "Who am I cleaning for, anyway? There is no fucking vicar!"

Rake's corpse-like stench churned her guts and, as she lunged out to push him away, the old boy lost his footing, flailing his arms as his body smashed onto the stone-tiled floor. Gem stared down at the motionless skeletal frame, fresh blood forming a ruby-red pool beneath his head. Time stood still.

In a hesitant shuffle, Gem grabbed her oversized coat, threw a few things in a bag, including the money she had accumulated from the cleaning job, and left the house.

Chapter 4

Gem walked and walked until her legs ached, the dull thud of Mr Rake's head hitting bare tiles playing over in her mind. With no concept of time or the distance travelled, light from a café window in the distance was a welcome sight. She was desperate for a warm drink and to take stock of what had just happened and why. The freedom she had so desperately craved had been inadvertently granted, and yet she hadn't bargained for the gut-wrenching disposition of being entirely alone and clueless.

Rake had likely stumbled to his death, the ultimate price for trying to attack an innocent girl, though one false move and it could have been an entirely different story. Regardless of Gem's disappearance and the probable stiff on the kitchen floor, Hattie would pay no mind; she's simply drag the old man's bones into the garden shed and carry on, albeit without a life-prop to satisfy her every whim.

The café's waitress was surprised to see such a young girl out so late. "Haven't you got a home to go to young lady?" she said.

"Yes, I do, thank you," Gem replied.

"Fair enough. We close at eleven, that's all," she said, handing her the bill. Gem gave the lady a five-pound note and asked for a few small coins in the change for the telephone across the street. Good job she'd had the forethought to grab the Post-it note from the fridge door, on which Fran had written down her new contact number.

Gem slowly squeezed her way in through the booth door that was hanging from its hinges, her shoes sliding on the piss-soaked floor. The workings of a public phone would be the first of many new adventures, as was checking the area codes listed on the wall before dialling. Even though it was late in the evening, Gem just had to let it ring out in the hope that Fran would answer – and sure enough, an agitated voice broke the monotonous tone.

"Okay – so who's this at stupid o' clock?" she said, clearly miffed by the intrusion.

"It's Gem – I've, erm, left Lanebridge."

"What? Do you have any money?"

"Yes, a little."

"You'll have to get a train. You know Lanewood Station, right? Get a taxi or something. It's Flat 2, Beedon Court, NW11. I'll leave a key under the plant pot by the back door."

Gem managed to scribble down the address before the beeps, and with just enough time to read it back to make sure it was right.

Having barely left the village, Gem was already overwhelmed by the presenting world, marring the sense of freedom to move of her own free will. She stopped a passer-by to ask for directions to the train station and was pointed towards a bus stop, yards from where they were stood.

"Wait for the number twelve. The route ends at the

station, so you'll be fine."

Anything beyond Lanebridge was an alien pursuit, a consequence of living in virtual isolation. When the bus finally arrived, Gem followed closely behind the lady in front, who'd just paid the driver without saying a word.

"How much is it to the station?" Gem said, sweltering beneath her massive coat and holding out what little change she had.

He just took the money, slung it in the cash tray and handed her a ticket. As the bus shunted forward, Gem clung to the rail and edged her way towards the nearest seat by the window.

The giant clock in the station's main foyer struck midnight, its echoing clang accentuating the emptiness, but for the odd commuter passing to and from the main entrance. Gem approached the information desk to request a ticket for the next available train to London, holding the piece of paper with Fran's address up to the glass.

"That's Glover's Green, my love, so that will be thirty pounds," the lady said, through the speaking holes. "Take the steps down to the lower platform and wait by the yellow seats."

The train finally left Lanebridge, marking the end of one miserable existence, its gentle motion rocking Gem to sleep, her head pressed against the glass. In no time, or so it seemed, the jolt of hefty brakes woke her from what she assumed was some crazy dream of being journey-bound for London. She gathered her thoughts and took her place behind a stream of passengers, reaching into overhead racks for luggage. The first step onto a busy platform blew her mind, with its incessant bustle of activity all at once. Even the framed street maps dotted along the main walkway were confusing: simply stating 'You are here' was a little vague for a village girl.

A lady standing close was drawn to Gem and her obvious confusion.

"Can I help?" she said.

Gem took the crumpled Post-it note from her coat pocket to show the lady.

"Ah, that's not too far from here – go straight ahead and then take a left, and you'll see the street sign,"

Being only metres away from Fran's ground-floor flat hastened Gem's steps along the busy street, crawling with commuters and cars cascading up and down the lined concrete. It was a total utter mental chaos and a complete contrast to village life, where everyone knew each other and the merest sight of a stranger drew out the outcast claws.

Gem took the key from beneath the plant pot that stood on Fran's doorstep and entered as quietly as she could within a dark and unfamiliar place. There were blankets in a folded pile on the sofa, which she presumed had been left out for her to use as covers. No more Hattie, her breakfast gong and the many daily rituals that had been etched in Gem's psyche since childhood. A new awakening, if you will, a new page turned, and anywhere was better than *that house*.

The morning's subtle light bled through the slats of the blind in Fran's living room window. Gem hadn't really slept, but felt rested and at ease. Muffled radio tones and the gurgling of an old coffee percolator drew her to the kitchen, where Fran was busy preparing cups.

"Thank you so much for taking me in," Gem said.

"It's fine. So, you left the old witch – what happened?" Fran said.

"You wouldn't believe what I've have been through with that vile woman, and then she got me working for a creepy old caretaker at the church."

"Sounds like fun."

The subject was understandably dubious, given that Gem really had no idea whether Rake was alive or dead. Her sudden disappearance could be a mitigating factor. Whatever the outcome, she'd had no choice but to defend herself against the man's threatening and interrogative behaviour.

The estranged siblings had plenty to discuss, including their mother's impossible personality. Fran's recollection of the woman was interesting, to say the least, especially her supposed sudden amnesia. One particular day, and for no logical reason, Hattie claimed not to know Gem at all, like she was some waif who Malc had brought back home. Little did Fran know that their mother bore an incredible hatred for her younger sister; she had never looked close enough to realise its true extent.

"What *was* in that envelope you gave Hattie before

leaving for London?" Gem said.

"Ah, that – jeez, she threatened to shop me for the last heist, so I gave her the lion's share of the money."

"What was the last heist?"

"I did a house a few doors down – unpicked the lock and voilà, found wads of cash in the guy's bureau."

"Why so close to home?"

"Dunno. All I wanted was for her to notice me, and she knew it."

The depths to which Hattie would plunge were limitless and shameful, encouraging – rather than dissuading – Fran to break the law, and to her own end. It turned out that Gem wasn't the only one craving a real mother, as opposed to some drain rat with a million scores to settle.

The sisters talked for hours, gathering lost connections and raking over uncomfortable truths. Things turned distinctly sour when Gem made mention of Malc, their differing opinions clashing like duelling swords.

"He was never around and when he was he rocked up drunk, spineless fucking weasel," Fran said, lighting a fag to dampen the fluster.

"He was just weak and irresponsible," Gem said.

"Get you being so polite – don't you mean, fucking selfish?" Fran said.

There was no denying the man's countless weaknesses, including the pitiful number of parental visits he'd made since leaving the family home, and mainly under sufferance. In childhood, Gem judged by meek comparison – he wasn't physically and mentally abusive, so was therefore acceptable. Blaming her father would have only thrown petrol on the flames of an already raging fire.

Gem's new abode would be Fran's spare room for the foreseeable. It was quite small with countless boxes stacked in the corner, crammed with stolen goods: designer gear, perfume and jewellery. The stash was a poke-in-the-gut reminder of Fran's fractured adolescence, a rebel child who stole for unrequited pleasure.

"Why don't you just sort it all out?" Gem said.

"It makes me feel like trash."

"It was just a lark, right? No use living in the past," Gem said, contradicting her own philosophy.

"Nah – it's in here, always will be," Fran said, prodding her temple. "Anyways – take what you want. I don't need it."

Gem was detached from that particular ruse, and so was able to sift merrily through the lost-profit items, some with eye-watering price tags still attached. In the end, she chose a suitable dress and a few tops, a decent hairbrush and a tub of posh moisturiser, a subtle reminder of having left her father's birthday gifts behind, and the only material consolation.

The bathroom was bright white, with plush towels folded over a heated radiator and labelled bottles aligned in size order across the window ledge. It was pretty ordinary, but luxurious compared to the conditions she had endured for years. Button by button, she slowly peeled away Hattie's cast-off jumble sale rags that had been nipped and tucked to fit her zero size.

It took a while to adjust the shower tap to a suitable temperature, but then the water rained down like a silky cascade, beneath which she lathered her skin with rose-scented body wash, cleansing every open pore. Shampoo was an absolute luxury, and not some old bar of manky soap that left her hair endlessly dull and brittle. It was 'new for old' exchange, fusty skank turned fresh and clean young woman.

The full-length mirror was a true reflection of endless excruciating days – an ashen-skinned skeleton, like some cave dweller who had never seen the light of day. She took the new hairbrush and turned a fistful of tangles into smooth dark strands, a beautiful black mane caressing her shoulders. Bruising would fade, and gradual weight gain would strengthen her feeble constitution, but to exist without fear of being dragged back to *that house*, to sweat over a hot stove and perpetually stir her mother's coffee to dissolve every single fucking granule – that would be her true saviour.

Gem strolled back into the lounge, stripped down and redressed.

"What do you reckon?" she said, swishing full circle in her new 'swag' dress.

"Well, just look at you," Fran said, leading her towards the sofa.

"So, you're gonna need to earn some money, right?"

"I guess so. Got to start somewhere."

"So how would you feel about working with me – a bit of filing, tidying the office, stuff like that?"

"Sounds good – anything is better than working in that crumby church."

"Do you mean the one in the village?"

The *Lanebridge Holla* was a free rag that covered the story of when the church closed and it turned out the caretaker had been swindling the levy accounts. Soon after, the vicar mysteriously disappeared. Rumours were rife that Rake had done him in and buried his body in the graveyard.

"Was it never investigated?"

"Nah, I think the vicar was bent and so paid the old scrote to keep his mouth shut."

*

Any kind of job at Cork and Hammond, a digital media company in the beating heart of central London, was just peachy for someone on the bottom rung. Gem was slating strong coffee and quaking in her borrowed shoes, trying to comprehend the hike from insignificant to some girl who just happened to fall lucky.

Hey, don't you worry about anything. This is your life now – no more Hattie and her fucking rulebook.

Of course, there was no room for insecurities and piffle – all Gem had to be was grateful.

A group of well-groomed and smiley young interns gathered in the office to welcome Gem on her first day. As with the inner 'victim' psychology, such an embracing welcome felt a little uncomfortable within a 'décor-magazine centre-spread' stylish gaff with shiny floors and clean lines.

"Get comfy – you can start with recording paid invoices on the spreadsheet. Switch on the PC and I'll show you," Fran said, pointing to the desk of a former colleague who had been promoted to another floor.

The black leather chair made for a cavernous slump, as Gem tried to comprehend the workings of a little box that one apparently refers to as a 'hard drive'.

The office newbie is routinely assigned to the role of tea and coffee monitor, and Gem was in the staff kitchen, trying to memorise the various beverage preferences. A young guy drifted in who she hadn't seen before, which was hardly surprising on her first day.

"Where's mine?" he said.

"Er, sorry, you didn't ask," Gem said, blushing like a naughty schoolgirl.

"Hey, only kidding. I'm Mark, nice to meet you," he said, his pungent cologne stinging her nostrils.

"I'm Gem, Fran's sister," she said.

"And what do you do, apart from make tea and coffee?" he said, with a patronising lilt.

"I'm just helping out to start with," she said.

She lifted the tray of cups and, with both hands full, thought he might do the gentlemanly thing and hold the door for her to pass through, but he just stood, watching. Among the many personalities occupying the same space, there was always going to be that certain intolerable gimp who no one likes, so she could tick that one off the list.

With every outstanding figure in the right column and in datal order, Gem was sifting through desk drawers and found some coloured pens and paper. She began to copy-draw some images from a glossy magazine, using text and borders to form a mock advertisement. The hours soon passed, aloft on daydreams of one day becoming a successful artist, surprisingly herself with the makeshift creations. Fran wandered back into the office, her eyes widening at such beautiful artwork and with limited resources.

"Wow, tell me you did these?" she said. "I need some designs for a cosmetics company – I'll show you the spec and we'll see what you come up with, yeah?"

"What, are you serious?" Gem said.

"Absolutely. We've got some artists here who couldn't match that."

Gem was positively buzzing and looking forward to pursuing a basic college course to further improve her technique, as was Fran's suggestion. From nil credibility to mildly treading a lucrative path – whose life was this, she thought. Dan should be sitting here right now, looking up –and not down his nose – at a former conquest sprouting from a bed of weeds.

While admiring Gem's reorganisation of the spare room, a piercing scream filtered through the studded wall. A spider with a circumference of a small saucer had scuttled across the carpet, and Fran was dancing about as if the damn thing had dived up her skirt.

"I hate those spindly things … uh!" she winced.

"They can't hurt you," Gem said, laughing.

In total contrast, Gem was morbidly fascinated by the wiriest of God's creatures and was searching under the bed, hoping to find a replacement for 'Mr Legs', who had been unwittingly left to fester in her old bedroom.

*

A bank account was a basic employee requirement, and so Gem was tentatively making her way to the nearest branch, guided by a scrap of paper on which Fran had written down basic 'left/right' directions. She was the merest fleck, wandering the street among hordes of pavement surfers and those marching with purpose.

There was a substantial queue at the customer service desk, so Gem took her place in line, rehearsing what she had to say over in her head. She was finally called over to take a seat opposite 'Jane', as per her name tag, dressed in blue with a patterned neckerchief and kitten heels.

"How can I help you today?" she said.

"I would like to open a bank account, please," Gem said.

"Savings or current?" Jane said, sounding a little facetious, as it was most unlikely for such a young girl to be investing money.

"Not sure. I've just started a new job," Gem said.

"Current it is," Jane said, tippy-tapping the appropriate selection on her computer keyboard. "Do you have any form of ID – birth certificate, driving licence?"

"I only have this," Gem said, handing her the Cork and Hammond confirmation of employment letter.

"I'll just be a few minutes," Jane said, staring at the piece of paper on which Fran had written down the relevant details, including a date of birth and temporary address – the only proof of Gem's existence.

Gem sat quietly watching other customers as they shuffled their way to each cashier point like cattle to slaughter, and at one woman in particular, who was wearing a tweed hat and with skirt pleats beneath a burgundy coat. Gem's entire body froze at the sight of the Hattie lookalike, thinking she could just march over and start beefing about her sudden departure from Lanebridge. Turned out to be someone dressed in similar clothes to her mother that inflamed Gem's over-active imagination, instantly quashing her decision to cut and run. Jane eventually returned, holding various documents and requesting a signature to finalise the process.

"You will receive a debit card and separate pin number within five working days."

"Thank you," Gem said.

*

Mark passed by the office on a regular basis, each time glaring in through the large glass-panelled window. As Gem was alone, he decided to walk in and fill the room with stuffy chauvinism.

"So, this is where you live, *Gemima*," he sniggered.

"It's Gem, thanks," she said.

He proceeded to perch his ass on the corner of Gem's desk and grabbed her sketchbook, flicking through the pages with zilch enthusiasm. The man's demeanour was borderline threatening and socially inept, and neither trait invited any meaningful social interaction.

"This isn't your office Mark, get gone," Fran said, returning from the weekly meeting.

"Your slaves are getting younger," he said.

"Who is that guy?" Gem said.

"*That* is the director's 'weirdo' son," Fran said, wanking fresh air.

*

There was a random car parked outside Fran's flat and, judging by her exasperation, she wasn't expecting a surprise visitor. Gem had plenty to do, so she headed straight to her room, leaving Fran to deal with the uninvited. All seemed relatively calm until voices grew louder and more venomous.

"You owe me three grand, darlin'," he said.

"Well, I haven't got it," Fran said.

Gem heard thuds against the wall, as if the two were scuffling.

"What you got in 'ere," he said, snatching her bag from the sofa.

"Yeah, go through it if you want – you'll find fuck all," Fran said.

"I'll see *you* next week," he said.

There followed a sudden door slam, marking the man's swift exit, so Gem went to check that everything was okay. Fran was in the kitchen, de-corking another wine bottle and filling her glass to tipping point.

"Who was that?"

"Ah, it was just some old boyfriend trying his luck. Being good in bed is one thing, but that's all he ever was," she said, sipping the happy nectar.

Gem wasn't exactly worldly wise, but even she could work out that the man was after money, not sex. She was learning a lot about Fran, and it wasn't always good, clouding the sisterly friendship that Gem had been wishing for.

It was almost time to leave for work, but Fran was still in a flimsy silk dressing gown and slippers, dragging on a roll-up ciggie. Bank statements and overdue bills were strewn across the living room table, and she was banging on about figures not adding up, and so on.

"Do you remember when I was searching through Hattie's things, and you tried to tell me I was looking in all the wrong places?" she said.

"Yes. Why?" Gem asked.

"I need some cash, and fast."

"That guy yesterday, he was chasing a debt, right?"

"No, I just need to pay for this place, my overdraft, credit cards, you name it."

Gem knew for sure where mother stashed her valuables – a savings book, jewellery, and what she believed to be a considerable amount of money – but was more concerned that Fran's intention to steal them away could raise hellfire. What with Mr Rake's possible demise, blowing the theory that Gem had simply left home because she didn't like working for the old scrote.

"Look for a leather pouch in the third drawer of the

dressing table. It's Wednesday, so she'll probably be out with the 'Cross Dollies'," Gem said.

"Good job I still have a set of house keys, eh?" Fran said. "And who the fuck are the Cross Dollies?"

"Just some crusty old women from the church."

In double-quick time, Fran was all dressed, out the door and en route to the train station. She was keen, all right, just like Hattie had been when her father's inheritance cheque dropped on the mat. It seemed money was the answer to everything, including mismanagement of lifestyle and stupid mistakes.

*

The underground station was yet another blow to the senses, as Gem made her way to Cork and Hammond alone. A few stops on an overcrowded subway train, huddled together like battery hens in a coop, couldn't distract her from what Fran might discover back in Lanebridge village – and there was no guarantee that Hattie would be out. Gem had thought long and hard about the Rake incident, and whether the whole thing could have been orchestrated. The old boy had no real reason to call at the house unless Hattie gave him the go-ahead to do whatever he liked, "for a price".

The staff kitchen was the last room at the arse-end of the office building and as Gem wandered in to prepare the morning's beverages, Mark was by the window, as if he had been purposely waiting. She carried on regardless, washing cups and humming a tune to drown out the sound of his feet shuffling on the floor. The distraction was soon lost as he sidled up behind, placing his groping hands inside her dress.

"Here she is – Miss Gemima," he said.

"Please stop," Gem said, mindful of the rage building up inside.

"Come on – you're not in the country now."

"Just go away, or I'll scream the place down."

Maybe it was her youthful vigour or innocent vulnerability that drew her like a magnet to the testosterone-driven predator, but she'd certainly had her fair share of crudeness and intimidation, and so found it relatively easy to stand her ground. He stepped away, shrivelling his delusional belief of being instantaneously desirable to the female fraternity.

"Slut," he said, heading for the door.

She should maybe report the incident to a superior, if such a person existed, who didn't hang from his shirt tails, pandering to the hierarchy.

*

Fran's coat was back on the peg by the door as Gem arrived home. She walked into the lounge, praying there would be no probing questions to compromise her reason for coming to London.

"The old witch wasn't there, so I just grabbed the leather pouch and, erm, Daisy," Fran said, pointing to the ugliest but most lucrative of shit ornaments that was now perched on the sofa.

It had been a substantial theft, and one could only pray that Hattie didn't turn detective in order to find the prime

69

suspect – the daughter she had previously encouraged to steal for material gain, such was the bitter irony.

"And that's for you," Fran said, handing Gem a considerable wad. "You helped me get it, so it's only right you have a share."

It was scant compensation for the all the hateful abuse and consequential psychological damage caused, but at least it would tide her over.

Chapter 5

Fran had not been to work for several weeks, and rumours were rife throughout Cork and Hammond that she'd shacked up with the regional manager. Gem was beginning to think that her developing role as an apprentice designer within an outrageously competitive setting was now shot to shit, lost in translation. The sisterly reunion was also crumbling, and Gem felt pushed aside on every level. Fran's habitual penchant for the unfaithful, manipulative and downright useless among men left a demoralising trail, and it was to hell with everything else, including her quaking financial position. Hattie's influence was inherent, with Fran's loutish approach to life, and the fallacy that status and material gain was the key to happiness. Whatever happened to succeeding based on one's own merit, driven by honesty and integrity? Based on such an analogy, Hattie was simply reaping what she deserved. Funny, that.

The Clipper Café was just far enough away to lengthen Gem's return journey home by a considerable hour. She was sipping at the froth of a particularly generous cappuccino when her eyes were drawn to a notice pinned to the wall, advertising for a '*liv*e-in' waitress. It was very tempting what with Fran being incognito and oblivious to the man who had been making regular calls while Gem was alone in the flat, bellowing through the letterbox for overdue rent.

Gem walked over to the counter to speak with the wait

staff. The manager was already in her coat and about to leave when she invited Gem into the back office.

"Sorry to drop in off-pat, but I've seen your ad on the wall and wondered if the position was still available?" Gem said.

"It certainly is – I take it you are interested? I'm Jenny, by the way," she said.

There were numerous reasons, the most poignant being her dubious living arrangements, which didn't really figure in such a verbal application. Gem explained that she had no relevant skills pertaining to the job, and had a meagre employment history, consisting of a cleaning job in Lanebridge and a questionable art apprenticeship that was on now hold. Jenny appreciated Gem's 'no frills' approach and outlined the job spec, explaining that the wage would be menial as there was no rent, but she could eat at the café for free.

"Why is there no charge for the flat?" Gem said, as one would when living in London of all places.

"It needs maintenance and various repairs, by law, to be viable for tenancy – leaky sink, a few dodgy floorboards and a paint job, but nothing too serious, so there's no need to worry," Jenny said.

"Is it very temporary?" Gem said.

"The owner is away on business so won't be overlooking the property for at least six months to a year," Jenny said.

"Sounds great," Gem said.

It was just the ticket. A place of her own felt a little

daunting and yet exciting at the same time. She even declined Jenny's invitation to view the flat prior to drawing up an agreement, preferring to go with her gut. And with that, it was arranged for her to move in the following day.

The fear of becoming homeless was now over, and all Gem had to do was find a suitable bag to throw in what little she owned, and a few extras from the swag pile, for good measure. She left Fran a note with a forwarding address and a loose apology for jumping the company ship, in case she returned before the landlord changed the locks. There was no way Gem could thrive in a job without guidance and support, and she sure as hell wouldn't miss Mark's creepy moves.

The side-entrance door of the Clipper had been left off latch so Gem could enter without pestering the wait staff for the keys. There was a considerable flight of stairs towards the flat's internal door, and as she stepped in for the first time she stood to take stock of her new surroundings. The walls were ruby-red, with a dark wooden floor and a table pushed to the wall, leaving a pathway towards the bedroom. The galley kitchen was particularly narrow, accentuated by several black cupboard doors on either side. Gem took down the ragged net curtain from the smallest of windows to let in a little more light, despite the outside view being a solid brick wall.

"This will do nicely," she said.

The layout was incidental – it was home, for now.

Polly, a fellow art and design student, had arranged to meet Gem for drinks at a local bar, mainly to talk shop about collage and other innocuous shit. Alcohol was a new venture for the freshmen, and Gem was gulping cider like it was about to expire, while Polly remained sensible, trying to keep a lid on her consumption. Despite being at either end of the affluence scale – Polly residing in a luxury apartment in Kensington with boyfriend, Teddy, and Gem in a flat above a corner café – the pair got on like the proverbial house on fire.

Mid-convo about aligning projects, an unmistakable voice hollered from the distance: "Fancy seeing you here, *Gemima*."

Gem scanned the bar area for Mark and saw the lowly creep among the crowd, swigging a glass tumbler of whisky and rye. She was about to yell some innocuous insult, but reined her neck in so as not to aggravate the situation further. Rejecting his advances was unacceptable in his book of fantasy fiction, and so wanted her head on a spike.

"We have to leave," Gem said, necking what was left of her cider.

"Why, what's wrong?" Polly said, puzzled by the sudden about-turn.

"Don't look up, but there's a man here who's been harassing me at work – I just can't stay," Gem said.

Their saving grace was the flat being only a short distance away, and Gem was already poised with keys in hand, ready to make a quick entry should they be followed. Walking along a deserted street heightened the creepiness as they both scurried back in silence, listening for nearby footsteps.

It wasn't the ideal finale to what had been a wonderful evening, and once home, Gem apologised for cutting it short, telling Polly all about the attempted assault in the staff kitchen.

"What a loser – you did report it?" she said.

"No, what would be the point – he's the director's son, for God's sake," Gem said.

"That doesn't matter. If that's his game, they'll all know all about it – these things spread like warm butter."

She was right: letting it slide wasn't a good move. The situation was already on tenterhooks with Fran's disappearance, which was why she quit the art job.

"Anyway, I shouldn't really be drinking," Polly said, patting her abdomen.

"What?" Gem said, wearing an exclamation mark.

"My period's a few weeks late," Polly said.

"Ah, but that happens all the time," Gem said.

"It's okay, I want to be pregnant," Polly said.

The surprise motherhood announcement came as a surprise for a girl who was quitting midway through an art college education. Plus, she was very young, and Gem couldn't hold back on the cynicism, wondering if it would still be the case if she and Teddy were living in some one-bedroomed council flat, surviving on welfare and hand-me-downs.

The café's morning shift was about to start and Gem was still catastrophizing about the previous night, and what might have happened if she and Polly hadn't left the bar so soon. And what if Mark turned up at the café to further antagonise the situation? Obsessing over the shifty behaviour of perpetrators and sex pests simply didn't figure in this new chapter of her life, and wished she could cut it loose.

Gem was wiping down the counter when a woman, and who she assumed was her daughter, came in and sat at a table by the doorway. The sense of disharmony was repulsive, and Gem recoiled as she walked over to take their order.

"Do you want me to come back in a little while?" she said.

"You may as well – *she* doesn't know what she wants," the woman said, glaring at the sheepish little girl opposite.

Gem returned to the counter, wishing they would just leave.

"It's okay, babe, I'll go over in five," Rache, her fellow café assistant, said.

From the cheap pearl necklace to her stupid 'granny' shoes furnished with white plastic bows, the woman made Gem's teeth itch. She peered through the glass pastry shelves at feet that were repeatedly kicking the little girl's shins beneath the table. Rache was about to go over and have words about the fracas when the woman got up from her seat, shoving the little girl towards the door.

"We shouldn't have come here," she said.

"No you shouldn't, scumbag," Gem said.

Jenny was wading through the café accounts when Gem decided to take a breather in the back office.

"You okay?" Jenny said, removing her glasses.

"Ah, it's just me being sensitive and all," Gem said.

"Was it the woman and daughter?" Jenny said.

"Yes, how did you know?" Gem said.

"She's been coming here for years and does exactly the same thing each time – she used to bring her son, and now that poor girl."

"Has no one reported it?"

"Yes – I have, even took a photo once. Nothing."

Gem had come to realise that the twists and turns of everyday life would likely be trigger-gut reminders of her past, like she was the one being abused all over again.

*

College homework kept Gem busy most evenings, which was just as well as she had no television and didn't read books, even though she wanted to. Hattie's money had been put to good use with the purchase of a personal computer and all the relevant software to help with research and enhancing her designs. With no telling of where it could lead, Gem had taken the liberty of emailing some artwork to a former Cork and Hammond client, whose contact she had noted down before leaving. Having already had one toe in the door of such a cut-throat industry, it would have been foolish not to.

The kitchen table was sprawled edge to edge with the arty contents of Gem's portfolio when a substantial spider appeared from within the paper layers, stopping dead as if to assess the texture beneath its legs. She placed a glass over the arachnid, watching as it tried to negotiate the smooth transparent dome.

"You can stay right there while I pop to the supermarket," she said, as if the critter could perceive logic.

*

Shallow footsteps and a whispered recital of a brief shopping list punctuated the stillness of a deserted street. The convenience store was an Aladdin's den, selling everything from shoelaces to exotic fruit, but she just grabbed what she needed and paid at the self-serve. It was raining heavily, so she ran back across the road towards the flat's side exit, when, during an awkward key-turn, a hand appeared from behind her head and pushed the door open.

"Up you go, *Gemima*, there's a good girl," Mark said, his husky breath dampening the nape of her neck.

That menacing tone was unmistakable, and even more so in a confined space.

"Why are you like this – what the fuck did I ever do to you?" she said, trying to bargain with the devil.

"I always get what I want -you should know that by now," he said, forcing her through the flat and towards the bedroom.

His bulky frame pinned her down on the bed, trapping

her arms beneath her torso. While fiddling with his zipper, she managed to twist and writhe enough to scream her lungs dry, and as she rolled over she was met with repeated fist punches pummelling her face.

"I fucking hate women like you," he said.

The world slowly faded, as did the pain, leaving a nasty metallic taste of blood in her mouth. Subconsciously, she was back at *that house*, surrounded by Hattie's derisory laughter. Until … blackness.

With one eye barely open, she tried to fathom her post-conscious state. The room was hazy and reeked of that familiar pungent cologne, inducing tears and self-pity. Gem managed to drag herself over to the side table to access the telephone, all the while praying that Mark was truly gone and not just hanging around to finish her off. It was the craziest thing to be ringing emergency services for herself – was she ill enough, suitably injured, and how would she describe what had just happened without puking?

"Yes, I am breathing. Please could you send an ambulance – I have just been attacked."

*

Flickers of movement and general muffle roused Gem from a drug-induced slumber, her head aching and heavy.

"Hello, lovie, can you hear me?" a nurse said.

Gem seemed lost, unable to comprehend the words, as if her ears were wrapped in cotton wool.

"Only just. Am I okay?"

"Yes, sweetheart, but you were very badly beaten. The

police will be coming to take a statement later, so you must tell them everything."

"Did I need any stitches?" Gem said.

"Thankfully, no."

As the various painkillers gradually wore off, flashbacks of Mark's physical invasion flooded Gem's head, each one a crippling visual assault. Such vengeful hatred could have taken her life and all because of an unrequited fumble in the office kitchen. Respecting a woman's dignity is far more alluring than any kind of expectation. Fuck men, she thought.

*

Mark, as the privileged son of a managing director, had access to some of the best lawyers in the city, on hand to fix his misdemeanours – while the victim had nothing more than an accusation, with no proof. It was only natural to question her moves that night – should she have gone out alone so late in the evening, when the only access back in was the flat's side entrance, concealed from public view? He could have been watching her for weeks, lying in wait for the perfect opportunity.

News of the attempted rape had filtered through the walls of Cork and Hammond, but when the actions of a prominent employee could potentially compromise a company's reputation, many just kept quiet. Fran was one such individual who had been burying her conscience in the accumulative backlog until prompted by 'a colleague' to do the right thing. She reluctantly took time out to visit the café and offer a piss-poor explanation as to why it had taken so long to acknowledge her sister's injuries.

Jenny just happened to be serving a customer when Fran arrived, acting as if all was well.

"You better come through," Jenny said, leaving Rache in charge.

"I, erm, just wanted to offer my sympathy – Mark, eh, the dirty bastard,"

"And that just makes it all okay," Jenny said, dying to rip off her head and kick it through the streets like a punctured football.

To dig an even bigger hole, Fran went on to further describe Mark's shady reputation as a womaniser, creeping around young blood like he was on home turf. She was fully aware of his unhealthy interest in Gem, but had been otherwise distracted, lost between the loins of the regional manager.

"What can you do, eh? Mark is up there with the rest of them," she said.

"It's a corporate cover-up and you are part of the problem – attempted rape is *not* acceptable," Jenny barked. "Anyway, shouldn't you be at the hospital?"

Fran gagged on Jenny's words, like piss from a darkened sewer, with no discernible excuse to evade the issue.

"I best get gone, then," Fran said.

Of course, they both knew that it wasn't going to happen. Instead, Fran took the bus straight back to Phil's house, lured by her craving for sex, material gain and whatever else went on in the woman's vacuous mind.

The police arrived at the hospital to take a statement, a necessary evil that stole Gem's reality. She couldn't help fretting that the incident had simply flagged up the whereabouts of a young woman who had fled from the exact address in Lanebridge where an elderly gentleman had been found dead.

"You have company," the nurse said.

A female constable and fellow detective inspector drew up some chairs to sit by her bed. With notebooks poised, they requested she run through the sequence of events as she could best recall. Gem took a sip of water and a few deep breaths before describing her first encounter with Mark, the prelim to what eventually happened. His ice-cold, threatening persona and the sexual advances in the staff kitchen, as if she was there for the taking, were indicative of his general attitude to women. The stalking began at the bar where she and Polly were drinking, and then later followed by the main feature: a venomous cloud that was firmly etched in her troubled mind. The stinging aroma of cheap aftershave, breathy groans and sweaty, clawing hands all over her body made her retch, and the detectives were considerate in their delving, to avoid further mental trauma.

"He punched me over and over until I passed out. Believe me, I know what it's like to live with anger, and he brought so much hate into the room."

Mark had a considerable history of violence and sex crimes, and, thanks to a reliable witness who had come forward to offer a detailed description of him running away from the flat in a dishevelled state, the police had enough evidence to prosecute. Having a rich and influential father wasn't going to save the steaming turd's reputation this time.

*

Following routine X-rays, a cocktail of prescribed drugs to guard against any subsequent wound infection, and a staunch refusal to pursue post-trauma counselling, Gem was finally discharged from the hospital.

"I see your taxi's arrived," the nurse said, pointing to Jenny, who was waiting for Gem to gather her things.

"I wasn't expecting this," she said.

"Come on, let's get you back home," Jenny said, clearly moved by the mass of purple-black bruising and mid-healing lacerations distorting Gem's face.

The flat was like a crime scene, with obvious signs of a struggle: furniture strewn across the floor and bloodstains on the crumpled bed covers.

"The police wouldn't allow us to move anything, but we'll soon get this place sorted," Jenny said, apologising for the disarray, as if she were somehow responsible.

"Please – I am really grateful for your help, but I need to do this on my own," Gem said.

It wasn't so much a tidy-up as a ruinous reminder of why it had happened in the first place. Restoring physical normality was unremarkable, except for the consigning of soiled bed sheets to a black plastic sack. Gem hadn't expected the spider she had previously captured beneath a glass on the kitchen table to be still alive and moving around, probably wondering what the hell had happened. She lifted the tumbler, and it just stayed there, as if confinement were preferable. What price freedom, she thought.

Another cold cup of coffee sat festering on the lounge table. Gem was lightly dozing when a willowy female figure wandered in through the door and stood by her chair.

"Jeez," she said, wiping her eyes to get a clearer view.

"Hey, sorry to disturb and all," Fran said, clutching a box of chocolates flourished with a cheap satin bow.

"I must have left the door open," Gem said.

Fran could also be a little tactless, and was openly gazing at Gem's obvious facial injuries.

"For Christ's sake, look at you. I wasn't expecting ..." she said.

"A face like a pummelled grape? No, neither was I," Gem said.

There were several beefs to be had with the sister of seldom consideration – and being left alone in a flat that was about to be repossessed by a vehement landlord was one of them. Thank God for the waitress job and flat combo, voilà.

"I'm sorry, love, I am a total fuck-up – you should know that by now," Fran said.

"That doesn't make it right, fuck-up or not. You can't just wipe the slate," Gem said.

"Is there anything I can do – a takeaway, glam rags?

What say I buy you a telly?" Fran said.

"I'm good, thanks. Just leave me be."

*

It took several weeks for Gem to physically recover, pending her flagging mental health that was balancing on a knife edge, all of which prompted a change of heart regarding therapy. There were countless issues, the latest being an understandable mistrust of men, clouding her ability to move on. Flashbacks of Mark's emergence from the shadows on that unfortunate night had left her fearful of anything beyond the walls, prompting a replacement light in the walkway to illuminate every crack and crevice.

Jenny was always welcome, day or night, like the mother Gem had always wished for – opposed to some crazed and bitter lump of nothingness. She knocked quietly on the door before creeping in, so as not to intrude.

"Check this out," she said, laying the local newspaper down on the table. "It's the best news, don't you think?"

Prestigious design company sex predator arrested for attempted rape and other offences.

The article confirmed that Mark had raped ten other women, four of whom worked for Cork and Hammond. It smacked of an inside job as the case was already cut and dried. Maybe the directorship, who had been paying lawyers to defend him, had decided enough was enough and shopped the lad good and proper.

*

The counsellor's office was within walking distance from college, down some back alley that led to a courtyard of various office outbuildings. The journey on foot allowed Gem a little time to mentally prepare for what she had presumed would be an uncomfortable reveal – a psychological self-analysis in exchange for relative normality.

Gem entered the brown door, labelled 'Howson Counselling', and was greeted by a lady who asked that she take a seat in the waiting area. Random canvas abstract paintings punctuated the spaces between tiny windows, trying to avert the clinical feel, though did nothing to supress Gem's intense internal butterflies. Minutes seemed like hours until Angela appeared with an entirely casual approach, unconcerned about whether the client was stoical or mentally bewildered.

"I'm glad you came – please, follow me," she said, smiling.

They entered a small room with two chairs and a table, on which stood an open box of tissues and a vase draped with tired flowers.

"So, how are you feeling today?" Angela said, tilting her head very slightly.

"I'm tired of being a victim," Gem said.

"The aftermath of trauma is different for everyone, and while some are happy to pour their heart out from the outset, others need more encouragement to gain trust. Where do you think you are?"

"I don't feel that I have a choice – if I don't open up,

things will never change."

For the next hour, Gem unravelled the harrowing details of abuse she had endured throughout her childhood, from the first punch to finally exiting *that house*, purposely skating around the 'Rake' fiasco. Angela was unaware of the significant historical suffering – Mark's attack was merely the conductor, releasing an outpouring of bitterness that hadn't seen light of day until now. Gem was a counsellor's conundrum, for sure, and Angela suggested the standard allocation of sixteen sessions with an open end for more if needed. Gem agreed, as long as they could be taken in manageable, though not necessarily, timely, steps.

"The damage is overwhelming, of course – what would you say is the worst burden?"

"I pretend to be fine, while inside I am crawling on my hands and knees. I don't know who I really am. Does that make sense?"

"Yes it does – absolutely, which is why I am here," Angela said.

Journal entries were positively encouraged as part of the healing process in the therapeutic world. Noting down thoughts, feelings and expressions, significant or otherwise, was something Gem hadn't really done since moving to London. Talking openly for the first time proved to be more useful that she had imagined, if only to acknowledge her turbulent history to one other person rather than run from it like it was the bogeyman.

*

Charity bake day had arrived, and the café was thronging with customers crowding the counter for orders and takeaways. Gem hadn't worked a shift for several weeks and was a little irritated by the noise, wishing she could be more like Rache, scuttling about the place, working the milk frother to a frazzle.

"Who's that?" Gem said, her eyes darting to the old man in the corner by the window, donning a white suit and panama hat.

"No oydia," Rache said.

"Not seen him in here before," Gem said.

"Well, stop starin', he'll fink ya feincy 'im," Rache said, sniggering.

The man was like a white pebble in tarmac and stood out from the other customers, though he probably just happened upon the Clipper Café for light refreshment.

Gem had been willing the shift to end and was so thankful that her journey home was only a flight of stairs away. Jenny was stood at the top of the landing, talking to some regular handyman in blue overalls, standing over massive tool box.

"What perfect timing this is, Elis – he will be preparing the property ready for sale," she said.

Gem's face must have drained to a shade of milky white, having clean forgotten about the preliminary conversation with Jenny prior to moving in.

"Don't worry – like we discussed previously, it's going to take a while," Jenny said.

"Would you like me to come back another time?" Elis

said, his eyes feasting on Gem as if she were breakfast.

The flirtatious glare was a little awkward, and she felt like the proverbial slab of meat in a butcher's shop window. Gem had grown incredibly sensitive and touchy towards any kind of male attention, and was therefore unable to differentiate between genuine interest and the downright salacious.

Talk of impending renovations had stirred Gem's propensity to obsess about her future. Falling on a job that came with rent-free accommodation had been a considerable find, making a backup plan virtually impossible with limited finances. She could flat-share, but even with split rent the cost would be far too high. Maybe it was time to ditch college and take up another position, to avoid another unviable situation.

Jenny had left an envelope on the kitchen table, and Gem was immediately drawn to the forwarding Knightsbridge address on the reverse side. The dinner invite from Fran and Phil was a flamboyant affair, typewritten in sugary scroll – craving a privileged status, with one foot in the dirt. She had no idea what to wear and didn't really own anything worthy of a soiree except the one dress from Fran's swag pile.

Regardless of Gem's lack of desire to suitably dress for the occasion, there was still a shortage of suitable clothing in her wardrobe. Polly's mother owned a backstreet clothing store that was only a few blocks away and also offered a generous discount to students – an obvious choice for her frugal budget. Gem did some considerable sifting before making her way to the changing room with several tops and jeans, hoping that something would fit. She was so damned skinny, even the smallest size hung over her like she was some sort of coat hanger.

"You found what you were looking for?" Mona said.

"Yes, I think so," Gem said, handing over her student discount card.

"You're Polly's friend, right?" Mona said.

"Yes, she told me about the store. Love the selection, and the maternity wear," Gem said, raising her eyebrows.

"Yes, it's a new line – I'm surprised you even noticed," Mona said.

Gem left the store with her wares in a carrier bag, wondering why her indirect reference to Polly's pregnancy went by the wayside. She had made the general assumption that all mother and daughter relationships, apart from her own, were pretty standard and so would naturally share such news – clearly not.

*

It was the first post-dusk outing since leaving hospital, and Gem was feeling a little jittery about the impending bus ride to Fran's place. She chose a seat near the driver and tried not to obsess about the prior intentions of every male passenger and focus instead on the magazine that was bought especially for the journey.

Gem reached her destination some twenty minutes later, and stepped off the plate into some 'picture postcard' scene, dotted with palatial houses, pea-green lawns and sprawling trees. The given directions led her to the very end property – an Elizabethan-style Renaissance home was jaw-droppingly elegant, fronted by massive iron gates that drifted open onto the gravelled pathway. The 'Queen of the Castle' was waiting, arms outstretched as if she hadn't seen Gem in years.

"Bet you thought we'd won the lottery," she said. "At least we're on the ground floor."

"So happy for you, sis," Gem said, the frivolous words contradicting her true feelings.

In truth, it was a real 'kick in the head' reminder of what exactly had replaced their relationship.

Phil was wrestling with a corkscrew, glancing up briefly to acknowledge Gem's arrival.

"Hey there, how are you?" he said.

"Come on, I'll show you the lounge," Fran said.

The spacious living room was oak-panelled, with a considerably large stone-built fireplace. Fran perched on the far side of a green velvet sofa, with Gem at the opposite end, subconsciously reflecting a tinge of hostility. News of Mark's conviction and the dismal shadow it had cast over Cork and Hammond's senior management made for a perfect frosty opening.

"What about the creepy guy, he got what he deserved, don't ya think?" Gem said.

"Ah, yes, what a wanker," Fran said, lighting a half-spent joint. "Can I tempt you?"

"No, I'm fine, thanks."

"So, how's the café?"

It's doing well – the flat should be ready for either sale or rent within the year."

"Well, you can always come live here if it all goes south," Fran said, with pupils like marbles.

"Thanks, but I'm hoping it all works out."

Ganja smog filled the room as Fran rambled on and on about life being a bitch, seriously.

"So, what did you do with that money I gave you?" she said. "Did ya spend it all?" She side-blew smoke from her parched lips.

So outrageous was the question, from a resident of a five-star luxurious flat in Knightsbridge, Gem nearly blew a gasket.

"Yes, as it was intended," Gem replied. "And anyway – you know how hard it is to survive in London, right?"

Gem's lot was far from lucrative, residing free gratis in a glorified bedsit above a café where she worked for a minimal wage and still, Fran was curious about what she had left, presumably to further bleed her sister dry. The ensuing pause seeped into the pores of the inciter, overriding the conscience of she who wasn't the least bit apologetic.

"I know I'm greedy, can't help it."

"You need to wake the fuck up – take a look at this place."

If avarice outweighed reality, it didn't really matter whether or not you had everything: the man, the wonderful home and a high-ranking job within a successful business; satisfaction became an unachievable goal.

At last, dinner was served, and Gem took her seat at the rectangular table between Lord and Lady Muck of Pretentious Manor. She felt a little substandard in her student-discounted jeans and shirt, but materialism masks a shallow individual, like throwing a velvet sheet over a pile of trash.

"Tuck in," Fran said, pointing to the freshly steamed vegetables in ornate china bowls, to accompany the fine fillet steak that was resting on her oval plate.

"This looks lovely," Gem said, salivating.

Minutes in, and Fran was already itching for more wine. She brushed past Phil's chair on her way to the kitchen and planted an insipid kiss on the back of his head, a pitiful gesture, belying her supposed attraction for the prize cock. Alas, could this be no more than a token relationship to align a wonky picture?

The meal was rich and wholesome, and Gem was already stuffed to the gills, with dessert to follow. The hosts were slowly drowning in copious wine refills, oblivious to Gem's 'ciggie break' stare through the nearest window. Phil had said very little since she arrived, apart from obligatory gestures to 'make nice'. Maybe he was sore, and considered Gem partly responsible for the company director's absence following his son's prison term, thus delaying a management tête-à-tête. God forbid, abhorrent crimes and consequential damage should get in the way of promotional accolades.

"So, now that you have left the company, what are

your plans going forward?" he said, like bait to a passing fish.

"College, and then we'll see – I really don't know at this point," Gem said.

"So, why *did* you go?" he said.

"Fran was my mentor and then she, er, kind of disappeared?" Gem said.

"Anyways, it doesn't matter now – you've moved on, babe, so now we can all chill," Fran said, trying to diffuse a situation for which she was entirely responsible.

The unlikely gathering had reached stalemate, with a festering bitterness that was homing in Gem's sensitive heart. Fran was unreachable and one coaxing shot away from being dependent on what she frivolously called 'recreational fun'.

"Well, it's been great, but I don't want to miss the next bus," Gem said, paving her way towards the door.

"Well, safe journey home, hun. Keep in touch, yeah?" Fran said, as they walked the winding path towards the iron gates.

The sibling bond never really stood a chance, but there had been lessons learned. Fran was a chip off the old block, 'nil of conscience' and another casualty of living with a mother who didn't know how to love anyone.

*

Another therapy session was looming, and Gem had planned to write a considerable journal entry prior to seeing Angela again. Her circumstances were vastly different, and the desperate need to fill many a twisted page with angry scroll was no more, making the process harder to adhere to. But while, as ever, childhood memories stung like fiery needles, there was still work to be done.

Gem had spent the night on the sofa and woke to find her journal face down on the floor and Elis in the kitchen, muttering something about dodgy pipes under the sink. Entering the flat uninvited wasn't acceptable, no matter how many repairs were pending. This was an invasion of her personal space.

"Sorry, looks like I am a little early," he said, smirking at her dishevelled hair and half-open dressing gown.

"Yes, you are," she said disapprovingly. "Could you maybe come back at lunchtime – I'll have gone to college by then?"

The poor guy's face dropped at the thought of rearranging his seemingly unadjustable schedule, so Gem caved in as long as he kept the noise down.

With that he rolled up his sleeves. "Tell ya what, I'll fill the kettle, seeing as I'll be turning the water off to fix the plumbing," he said.

Fiddling with interconnecting pipe joins and the inevitable clanging of tools made it impossible for Gem to write anything. Delving into one's own headspace definitely required solitude.

*

The college bus was due and Gem ran across the busy road while rooting through her purse for the appropriate change.

"See you later, gorgeous!" Elis yelled out from the

café doorway.

Fellow students sat by the window, sniggering at the sight of some guy in overalls, waving Gem off with an oily rag. The roving pursuit of a reasonably attractive man would be just fine if she were ready to have her heart plucked out and pumped up like an old cushion. Such a prospect was too scary to contemplate, preferring solitude to any kind of pairing.

Polly was waiting outside the main gates, glancing at her watch and looking exasperated. "Come on, we'll be late for class," she said.

Gem apologised for being on the last push, her thoughts firmly pinned on the afternoon's impending therapy session. The classroom was buzzing, oblivious to Mr Sellers, whose patience gave way to a fist-banging prompt on the blackboard. "Can we all just please *sit down?*" He was a little oddball, and Gem liked his non-curricular style that didn't always fit neatly structured boundaries. The task was to recreate a piece of art of their own choosing, and as Gem was trying to think, a spider was slowly making its way across the desk and into her pen box. The one piece that sprung to mind was a shitty canvas abstract that hung above the fireplace in Hattie's living room, resembling a paint mass apologetically splayed out to form a dodgy horizon. Gem selected random colours and dashed them in unison across the paper, punctuating the baseline with vague impressions of trees to separate land and sky. Polly's freehand rendition of *The Scream* wasn't the best choice and hard to capture using acrylic pens.

"I should have picked a Picasso," she said, giggling.

"I thought you already had," Gem said.

*

The counselling consultation room was different to the one previously, with no flowers on the table and an empty tissue box. The window was slightly open, allowing a gentle breeze to pass through the blind slats and cool the stuffy air.

The discussion began with an apology for Gem's missing journal entry, like some schoolgirl who had forgotten her homework. She fumbled with her cardigan buttons and began to cry, talking between sobs about self-doubt and how the past had shaped her beyond recognition.

"This fucking slab of paper poison is just a ruinous reminder of what I once had to do, like a trigger poke in the gut," she said, slamming the journal down on the table.

"Use it or burn it – there are no rules," Angela said.

"I am in denial, that's the truth. If I write it down, I can't escape it."

Fair point – the emotional biop mirrored the negotiation of each tentative stepping stone across a river of crocodiles in pursuit of dry land, a torrid and often backward process. She just wasn't expecting demons to show up for dinner.

There had been little mention of her father during therapy, as was purposeful or 'avoidant' in textbook terms. Acknowledgement of his virtually non-existent presence during childhood was a raw admission, as the truth became clearer with age: the man was just a spineless, willowy shadow who had continued on with his own life, allowing Hattie's repellent sting to destroy everything, including the vaguest of parental connections.

"Let's face it, he probably never loved me," Gem said.

"He needs to know what his complacency has done to you," Angela said.

"Well, I don't even know where he lives."

"Your sister might?"

"Sadly."

"You sound very opposing."

"She's just another disappointment. She was a stranger to me when we lived at home, and now that I know her, she's just not what I expected her to be."

The need to belong, to be coveted, is the child in all of us – and Gem had pinned all hopes on Fran being that person, forgetting that she, also, was a victim of an abusive mother, the consequences of which were now unfolding.

"What is your fondest memory of your father?"

Gem stopped for a while, to consider the true meaning of the word 'fond'. While she had always felt love and empathy for the man, he remained void of emotion. His kisses were cold, the hugs were reticent and awkward and the only time he smiled was as he was leaving the house.

"I don't have one," Gem said.

The session drew Gem to a poignant conclusion, that

she must make a conscious decision to protect herself, disallow those who sought to, or had done, insurmountable harm, to dictate her self-worth. Poor mental health would only breed further insecurity and unhappiness; like water left in a glass, over time it would grow cloudy from the build-up of atmospheric dust particles. Outlook changes everything – and therapy was metaphorically replenishing rather than neglectful.

*

Once again, Gem boarded the bus to Knightsbridge, thinking she may as well, as it was closer now than if she were travelling directly from home. She could have called Fran about her father, but a discussion was needed if only to filter out the bullshit. This time the journey was noisy, with a bus was full of public school fodder poncing about on the back seats, such that it was hard not to scream at the stupid fuckers to pipe down.

The gates of 'Fancyville' slowly opened onto the widening pathway, and Gem could see Fran waving in the distance.

"Miss me, did ya?" she said, puzzled by the impromptu visit so soon after the first.

They walked into the lounge, where a half-spent joint was perched on the ashtray, burning an ash trail.

"Been busy?" Gem said.

"Always busy, hun," Fran said, sweeping her matted hair up with a plastic slide.

"You're wired – what the hell do you put in those smokes?" Gem said.

"It's just a bit of weed – it helps me chill," Fran said, taking another substantial drag.

"What else is one to do while Phil lashes the ball on the golf course and dinner braises in the slow cooker, except reach for a convenient prop to numb the senses?"

"I need my father's address," Gem said.

"What? Have you lost your mind?" Fran said, while flicking through the contacts on her mobile phone. "Why do you bother with the useless drain rat?"

"Dunno – I could ask you the same question," Gem said.

"Well, this is my old phone – it needs a fucking enema," Fran said.

Gem's reasons for getting in touch with her father were her own, even though Fran may well have had a valid point. The answer was both complex and straightforward – Hattie had been a considerable influence, but to what extent did he really care about his own flesh and blood?

"Hattie and Malc, eh? What a pair," Fran said.

"I barely saw them together."

"Surprised they didn't kill each other."

Being the older sibling, Fran talked some more about their dysfunctional relationship and the endless bitter conflicts and angst. They would have arguments at the dinner table, and Hattie would instigate debates about why they never had sex, openly ranting about his erectile dysfunction. She was totally repellent and would throw things across the table, so Malc would just get up and leave, sometimes for days at a time.

"Awkward," Gem said.

"Yeah, I used to take you to your bedroom. You didn't need to listen to that shit."

*

Gem returned to an empty flat, just as she left it, with no sign of Elis and his work-laden tools. Not only had he wiped the sink, cleaned the cups and put them back in the cupboard, but had also a scribbled note, left on the table: 'See you soon gorgeous x'. What's with the kisses, she thought – they barely knew each other, and he was already flirting on paper.

Chapter 6

A single email sat in Gem's inbox, titled 'Interview Invite', and with trepidation, she clicked to open up the message from the digital art and design company where she had previously submitted her image portfolio. They wanted to discuss a prospective role at the main office and she had just one week to create some new designs and illustrations.

There was also the impending construction of her father's letter, a literary spillage of emotion that had been gnawing at her soul. How the hell was she meant to express the heart-rending pull of a questionable father-daughter relationship with a cheap biro? 'Dear failed protector – tell me why you left me with one hellish and sadistic mother, knowing what she was capable of.' A response was her only hope to enable partial forgiveness, or else she'd loathe the man until her last breath.

Rache had rung in sick, so Gem was working in the café alone, at least for the morning shift. During a quiet moment she took out her pen to add more detail to the letter, staying concise, to the point. "That's it – no going back," she said, sealing the envelope.

The white-suited man was already sat in the corner, holding a cup of espresso – which was bat shit weird, as the coffee machine wasn't even switched on and was still squeaky clean from the day before. As he glanced over to the counter a feeling of complete serenity stole Gem away, like she'd been snorting Fran's ganja. As the delirium faded, she found herself questioning why she was standing behind a counter, holding a waitress pad.

"Are you okay?" Jenny said, having drifted through to check the menus.

"Yes, sorry. I was just feeling a little dizzy – it's gone now."

"You should grab a bite to eat while the place is still empty."

Gem looked back at the table in the corner, and it was empty, with the chair tucked underneath. If she wasn't going completely mad with her imagination in overdrive, then the white-suited man must have either floated through the wall or passed through the door without activating the café's doorbell.

Lost in the lingering words of solemn non-fiction and a slight fuzziness, Gem was about to close up the café when Polly showed up at the door.

"Jeez, are you trying to scare me to death?" she said.

"I've been trying to call you. Wondered if you fancied going for a few drinks later – mine's definitely an orange juice, by the way", she said, flouncing her thickening waistline.

"Sounds like we have something to celebrate," Gem said.

"See you at the Cactus Flower around eight."

*

It was just the ticket, as Gem needed a meaningful distraction to get her head straight. Rummaging through her wardrobe, she found a few unworn items from Mona's boutique, the only good thing to come from Fran's dinner invite. As she laid the clothing down on the bed, she noticed a gold chain glistening from beneath the carpet fibres. Mark must have been wearing the diamond-encrusted black skull pendant when he dragged her into the bedroom – incriminating evidence that had remained undiscovered, despite a thorough police investigation. She placed it on the dresser because of its potential value and not because it meant anything – it might turn up trumps if she took it to some pawn shop.

*

The bar was reasonably quiet and Gem walked over to where Polly was sitting, guarding a suitably filled wine glass. She mentioned the interview – or rather a pensive discussion – and confessed to having poached the client from Cork and Hammond before leaving. Polly understood, as sometimes it's the only way to cut through in the art world – some would fight to the death to bag the chance of a lucrative contract.

"What about your career?" Gem said.

"On hold – I'll return to college at some point. Anyway, what are your thoughts on being the baby's godmother?"

"I'd love to."

"I saw your mum the other day."

"Was Dave there?"

"No, she was alone in the store."

Polly hadn't spoken to her mother for a good while,

saying that it had all been very different since Dave arrived on the scene. Gem tried not to dwell on her own twisted logic, secretly thinking that at least Polly had a mother, and keeping quiet about the pregnancy seemed a little harsh. Surely such an upcoming event was undeniably special, and Polly might need the support.

Talking of men, Elis's name inadvertently slipped from Gem's tongue, as the guy who was doing running repairs at the flat, and then she began to question why he would even figure in the conversation.

"And what do you think of him?" Polly said, with 'that look' in her eye.

"That's just the thing, I don't know," Gem said.

"Do you go all tingly when he's around?" Polly said.

"Do I what?" Gem said, laughing – or was it her avoidant nature?

"You can't fool me," Polly said.

*

Freehand drawing was one thing, but to create to order was off the scale, stressful and nothing like easy, especially when a job offer was hanging in the balance. Gem decided to take a break, slipped on her coat and trainers and headed off to the park for a casual stroll. The coffee stall was heaving with thirsty customers, and as she scanned the seating area she caught a glimpse of Phil, in deep convo with another woman. Naturally curious, Gem slunk past and behind some trees so she could take a closer look. This time they were sucking face, arms everywhere, clutching and squeezing. What to do, Gem thought: spill the beans and therefore incite another emotional avalanche, or just leave it be? Fran was needy, though not in a loved-up sense and would probably ignore the dalliance anyway, so as to keep the lifestyle to which she had grown accustomed.

*

Hours of work had finally paid off, and the portfolio was now fit for presentation. Gem was tidying and must have disturbed the spider that had previously crawled inside her art case during the last college lecture. The creature scuttled across the table and onto her hand, tickling her skin with the tiniest of steps.

"Where are you going?" she said, laying it back down on the table.

The hefty clunk of Elis's toolbox outside marked another impromptu house call. Gem wasn't entirely happy with him owning a spare key to the flat and made a mental note to speak with Jenny during the next café shift. After all, it was a Sunday, for God's sake, and Gem was still in her nightie and slippers.

"Hey, gorgeous, I won't be long – just dropping some parts off and then we can maybe have a cuppa?" he said.

"Help yourself, you must know where everything is by now," Gem said.

Once again, the intrusion was all-consuming: the kettle's hiss, clinking spoons, footsteps shuffling on the lino. So, Gem went off to get dressed, or else spoil her manners. It was probably an over-reaction, what with her head filled with the imminent Pineapple Indigo meeting, and she tried to focus instead on the countless days spent in isolation, when she had longed for anyone's company.

A mug of hot tea was waiting on the kitchen table. Elis had pulled up a chair, and was happily thumbing through Gem's portfolio.

"Hey girl, these are really good," he said. "I studied art at college and then someone told me you only make money as an artist when you're dead."

"I hope not – I have a job interview next week."

Regardless of the shallow banter, he did seem genuinely interested in the one aspect of her life that she *was* happy to share. The lad was a native Londoner whose father believed that fancy careers were solely for the upper classes, which was why he became a tradesman. It was weird how attitudes of past generations were still prevalent in the present day, that getting your hands dirty was still considered the mark of a true grafter, while office workers ponce about in white shirts and slacks.

*

There had been no response to Malc's letter, and Gem felt a little disgruntled with the situation, edging around the very mention of her father as if it would jinx it further. Angela tried to shift the view, suggesting she should maybe wait a little longer before assuming the worst, and give him chance to prove otherwise. After all, some men see parenting as an optional vocation, a rainy day pursuit, should one have nothing else better to do.

"Fuck him, anyway – I've come this far," Gem said.

"That's true enough," Angela said.

The interview was in a couple of hours and Gem was feeling understandably shaky, desperate to leave the Cork and Hammond initiation behind and start over. She left the flat a little early, just in case the bus was late or she couldn't find the building. Along the way, there was a café with seats outside and she figured a caffeine boost would help her to focus. There was always the head-punch of Angela's timeless cliché: "The only way is forward."

Pineapple Indigo's main doors slid open into a large foyer which led to a swish long-line reception desk. The set-up was sleek and ultra-modern, its décor reflective of the upmarket clientele. Following the usual check-in, Gem was directed to a row of modern bright orange chairs and a swanky white occasional table. The precisely stacked design magazines in the centre seemed more for ornamentation than reading matter, and so she just sat tight, watching people – like worker ants – shooting off in various directions.

At the exact time allocated, a tall guy in a neatly pressed suit came to greet her, his pose typical of the young managerial type, overseeing business from the comfort of a soft leather chair.

"I'm Theo – nice to meet you," he said.

She reciprocated, shaking clammy hands with someone whose decision could plot the course of her future employment.

"How are you today?" he said, to neutralise the

business vibe.

"I'm fine, thank you – just a little nervous," Gem said.

Gem followed him, clutching her portfolio in case it blew away in a gust of corporate wind. His office was obsessively tidy, books in size order, and evenly drawn blinds.

"Please, take a seat," he said. "Would you like a coffee?"

Her mouth was as dry as sticks, but thoughts of lifting a cup to her lips at a time of scrutiny was just too risky – what of drips or stains, and the minuscule chance of choking?

"I see you've brought your work – could I take a look?" he said.

"Yes, of course," she said, handing over the zipped black folder.

Each laboured page-turn seemed to last aeons, as he studied her designs every which way, occasionally glancing back to the previous plastic sleeve.

"So how is college going?" he said.

Gem explained that she was nearing the end of the initial art skills course and was thinking of enrolling for the second year. The way forward was an integral combination of acquiring first-hand experience that allowed time for future studies. "Your work is excellent, especially for someone so young, but you *are* still an apprentice," he said.

"Yes, but I believe that my passion to create defies my age," she said.

Theo skimmed through the portfolio once more before closing, his expression in no way reflecting the possible outcome.

"What are your thoughts regarding an internship with the company until you are fully qualified and then, if all goes to plan, moving into a full-time position?"

"That sounds fantastic," she said.

"So, we will see you on Monday to discuss a manageable timetable," Theo said.

Gem left the office, replaying the interview in her head, making sure she wasn't mistaken. The offer was a breath of rejuvenating air, sweeping away self-doubts as to whether she was a viable investment. Less opportunity to work in the café would be the forfeit, and Jenny would surely understand that her future came first.

*

A new coffee house had opened up a nearby, doling out freebies and discounts to entice prospective punters. The idea hadn't swayed the white-suited man, who rolled up as usual, this time walking straight to the counter to order.

"Nice to see you," Gem said. "Is it the usual espresso?".

Once again, his presence was invasive, like some hypnotic infusion, breeding an undeniable sense of anger and resentment. She made her apologies and wandered into the back office, unable to comprehend the sudden and unexpected outburst of repulsion, imagining her hands clawing at Hattie's flesh and screaming blue murder. This was in stark contrast to having been previously swept away in a cloud of mind-numbing tranquillity, like some LSD hit. The fleeting dissociation eventually subsided, leaving her pale and clammy.

"Seen a ghost, babe? White as a sheet, you are," Rache said.

"Where is he?" Gem said.

"Who's that, then?"

"The man who always sits in the corner."

"We're not open yet, babe."

Jenny eventually showed up late afternoon, following a lengthy visit to the accountant's office, and judging by her gleaming expression, things had clearly gone much better than expected.

"Can I have a word?" Gem said.

"Of course – I gather its good news?" Jenny said.

"Yes, I just can't work as many shifts, and that was my half of the deal."

"The flat would be empty without you, so it cuts both ways. Anyway, Elis isn't well – another MS flare-up."

"I didn't know there was anything wrong," Gem said.

"He'll be okay in a few weeks," Jenny said, sensing Gem's underlying sadness.

The unexpected announcement had quashed Gem's plan to avoid romantic relationships at all costs. Truth was, her heartstrings had been well and truly plucked the day he hollered from the café doorway, when she realised right there that *not* all men were the same. The fiery blush of an adolescent girl, all giggles and innocent fumbling, was now a young woman reluctantly falling for some guy she barely knew.

*

The new role was inspiring and enabled Gem to comfortably split her time between working and further education without juggling too many pennies. The only con was the exchange of a regular interaction with the Clipper Café staff for empty convos with fellow artists and designers. Most were slaves to their own agenda and would fight like dogs for the chance to feature in some high-end glossy rag. Gem was happy to be an apprentice, consigned to the role of tea monitor and occasional inspirational sponge, but in a position of her choosing.

Her desk was on the fourth floor, in a sectioned room of people at various career levels. Theo padded the office grounds on a regular basis, offering feedback, constructive criticism and the occasional reprimand should a certain person be on their third coffee break with no viable work on the PC screen. Gem had been given a test page spec for mascara, which meant drawing a hundred different pairs of eyes and an illustrative construction of the item itself.

*

An envelope was lying by the door as Gem arrived home. She had never seen her father's handwriting, but as letters were a dwindling form of communication, it just had to be his indistinct scroll. She tore it open with nil expectation, and pulled out an ink-stained tri-fold sheet of paper that looked like a former cup rest before being sent.

I have to t lk to you, but not lik t s. Can w get tog th r.
Phone me o the above num er. Dad

Shame it wasn't a more heartfelt response to her raw and intensive spillage that took hours to construct. Gem sat down on the sofa and dialled the number given, which rang out twice before switching to the briefest of voicemail greetings: "Hi, leave a message, ta."

"It's me – thanks for your reply. Meet me at the Clipper Café on Sloan Street, W1, this Saturday, around eleven," she said after the beeps.

The one-sided arrangement seemed a bit flimsy, especially as the man was historically unreliable and would sooner duck out than face the music. She tried not to obsess, staring at her phone for hours should he ring back to check or change the arrangements, blah …

Chapter 7

The smell of cooking filtered down the stairway as Gem entered the side entrance to the flat. She walked in to find a freshly laid table with fluted wine glasses and a bottle of fizz placed in the centre. Jenny was in the kitchen, preparing various ingredients and singing at the top of her lungs to some random song on the radio.

"What's all this?" Gem said, having counted three place settings.

"I figured we had plenty to celebrate, what with you starting a new job and all," Jenny said, smiling.

"So who's the guest?" Gem said.

"Elis, of course – he'll be along soon. I didn't think you'd mind."

"Of course not," Gem said, with a joyous heart. "Anyway, the kitchen tap still needs fixing."

She walked into the bedroom and jumped up and down on the spot, relieved and yet so incredibly nervous, having inwardly acknowledged her true feelings. What better excuse to slip into something a little less formal and to spruce up her pale cheeks with a dot of blusher?

"Let's hope he's worth it," she said to the mirror.

Shadows can be deceiving, and what appeared to be reflecting tree branches on the bedroom wall looked like the considerable sprawl of a spider's legs. To make doubly sure, Gem turned off the light to see if the outline remained, but there was nothing, not even a tree outside that would feasibly create it. The illusion left her a little creeped out, and she checked behind and under the bed, in every corner and around the drawer unit. She waited a while, just to see if whatever it was would crawl back, conscious that there were far more important things to attend to.

A homemade lasagne was resting on the oven top, and Jenny was prodding the middle with a fork to check if it was sufficiently hot.

"You look nice," Jenny said.

"She certainly does," Elis said, standing in the kitchen doorway, clutching a four-pack and a bunch of flowers.

Those eyes were already pinning her against the wall with a groin thrust, devouring her lips with rapturous kisses.

"Come on, you two, let's eat," Jenny said, shooing them both towards the table.

Elis had clearly lost weight, his pallor reflective of previous weeks, but Gem made no mention and continued as if she had seen him only yesterday.

"It's so glad to have you both here," Jenny said.

The evening was superb, filled with catch-up banter, smiles and laughter, thanks to Jenny, who had organised the surprise gathering. Gem was now fighting an emerging vulnerability – a shackle of 'love' that digs deep into your chest and tears your heart open wide – made harder still when she consumed alcohol.

"So, have you already burnt the college books?" Elis said.

"Nah, I might need them for another year. Depends on

the job," Gem said.

"Well, there will always be a shift for you here at Clipper," Jenny said, reassuringly.

"That would be great, but I take it things are about to change?" Gem said.

"Yes, we now have the money to expand, give the place a refit and maybe employ a few extra staff members," Jenny said.

Elis was warmed by the news, knowing there would be more work for him to do. Regular bouts of long-term illness could be a financial risk, and he didn't want to punch a considerable hole in his future just yet.

Whether it was apple pie and custard or a pot of gold filled with fifty-pound notes that Jenny had placed on the table, there was no distracting the lovebirds, and it was only a matter of time before the tumble crusade, tugging at buttons and undergarments.

"That looks lovely. I might have some later," Gem said.

"Well, that's me done guys, I have an early start tomorrow," Jenny said, walking towards the door with an all knowing look on her face.

An awkward silence followed, as Gem stood from her seat and began shuffling dirty plates to overt Elis's wanton stare and to gear up for 'the' moment of no return.

"Come here, you," he said.

"You're such a cad. What makes you think I want to?" she said.

"But I'm irresistible, right?" he said, laughing.

Their lips fused together, as they sidestepped like crabs towards the bedroom. The pheromone hit of masculine cologne and nervous sweat was arousing, as were his hands cruising every inch of her body. A 'let's hit the sack' sexual crescendo was a foregone conclusion as she quietly caved in for all the right reasons.

First light stirred many things: Gem's undeniable weakness for the guy who lay by her side, and emotive sex, and not just some juvenile romp that has zero meaning and ends before it even begins. She tried so very quietly to get out of bed, but Elis dragged her back: "Just another ten."

"I can't – I'm meeting my father."

"Okay – does he live in London?" he said.

"Somewhere Surrey way – I'll explain later," Gem said.

It was considerably bad timing and although there were no solid expectations, Gem was holding out for her father to do the right thing, to engage in a long-awaited discussion about their estranged relationship.

*

Gem ordered coffee from the fast-food joint that was directly across from the Clipper Café. She sat on a stool, looking out of the solid glass front, which was better than lurking in some skanky shop doorway. High on wishful thinking, she imagined Malc paving his way down the street, glancing at his watch like a scene from some nostalgic movie, before crashing through the clouds at the thought of a 'no show'.

"Filler?" a guy said to Gem, and her empty cup.

"Yes, why not?" she said.

The appointed hour came and went, as did another half hour and then some, at which point Gem left the burger bar with her face trailing on the floor. It was partly anticipated, though no less disappointing. She felt sick inside, watching as parents with children of all ages passed her by, happy to be together, as one. What in God's name had she done to warrant the shittiest of childhoods – a continuum of solitary, dark days, void of any fond memories to warm the soul?

To hide her weepiness from the café's wait staff, Gem sneaked in through the flat's side entrance. She had hoped to spend time alone, but Elis was in the kitchen, rinsing coffee cups.

"I thought you'd be out," she said.

"I'm still on phased hours, so what happened?" he said.

His genuine concern tore down her mustered composure, and she fell into his arms, tears flowing like a Texas flood. Her ravaged heart bled out – years of systemic maternal cruelty and a father who remained perpetually distant and oblivious.

"He wasn't there. What a fucking surprise."

"It's no consolation, but my mother left us when I was two – took off with the old man's best friend," he said.

Other kids' taunts in the playground could be so cruel, and were harrowing echoes to this day. Word had somehow spread that his father was a single parent, and for some inane reason was called a bastard, a shallow insult chanted by imbeciles who cared not for its real meaning or the anguish caused.

"Have you ever tried to find your mother?" Gem said.

"Hell, no – knowing that she could still be out there, living another life, is worse than if she were dead," Elis said.

Several hours of straight, 'no frills' talking and a few stealth vodkas into the evening, their disjointed worlds had been deconstructed and reassessed. Gem was free to feel, and it didn't matter whether she was sad, angry, bitter or regretful – she had found a podium on which to vent without reproach or justification.

*

The office was a welcome distraction from her delicate constitution. It was unusually quiet, such that Gem checked the wall planner to check for any missed meetings, until whispers and giggles filled the entire floor.

"What's this, guys?" she said.

"One of your designs has been accepted for a top magazine review – this is monumental," Jasmine said, showing her the layout. "We are so proud of you, and hey – great promo for Pineapple Indigo."

"Well, that's just the best news," Gem said.

*

Over time, expectations had finally been curtailed, and Gem was glad to be back at the café, working a weekend shift. Jenny was been busy, expanding the business with a broader coffee range and outsourcing pastries from individual suppliers, and Rache was happy to provide any training needed to use the new equipment, including a brand-spanking-new coffee machine. The counter and glass displays were now a little bigger, pending a complete refit later in the year.

"Well, blow me da'an," Rache said. "'E ain't been in 'ere for ages."

The white-suited man chose his usual espresso, despite an array of new continental blends and flavours, pointing specifically to the small cups that were stacked against the frother. Gem left extra complimentary biscuits on the saucer, to make up for deserting him at the counter previously, not that there was any malice – he just doffed his hat and walked over to his usual table in the corner.

The place had been ticking over like an old clock until Fran, with her dope-stance, stumbled in through the café door, cock-eyed on some ganja trip.

"Can I have a word?" Gem said, marching her disjointed sister into the back office, feeling so damned grateful that Jenny was out.

"What the fuck is this – you're steaming?" Gem said.

"I need some money, anything, please …" Fran said, like a random street beggar.

This had been a long time coming. All the 'cheeky fags' to stem the downward flow had finally claimed what was left of her common sense.

"You need to go home," Gem said.

"I can't. He's thrown me out of the apartment," Fran said.

"Why?" Gem said.

"Because *he's* a fucking arsehole, that's why."

Fran had gone home to find Phil in bed with some woman and freaked out, calling her a slut and shouting every insult in the book. At that point, Gem took the opportunity to fess up about seeing him cavorting in the local park, to further deepen the hole.

I wasn't going to tell you, but I suppose it makes no difference now," she said.

"I knew anyway – he's had no end of slags."

Shacking up with one's manager is a bad decision, especially if the man was savouring many cakes in toe-rag kingdom. Gem knew of a safe house nearby, so she called the police on Fran's behalf and concocted some story that she was fleeing from an abusive partner. It seemed the queen of acquired affluence had been stripped of her title, in exchange for a hostel piss pot.

A police car finally pulled up outside the café, and not down the side – which would have been much more discreet and away from prying eyes.

Gem gave Fran a carrier bag with some toiletries, underwear and a pastry selection from the counter to take to the refuge, and she quickly adjusted her skirt before climbing into back seat.

Afterthoughts can be enlightening, and there were a few things that didn't quite add up regarding Fran and her supposed sudden plunge into poverty. As a Cork and

Hammond employee, she would surely have had access to funds already earned, and anyone with a job was not technically destitute. Could it be that Phil had made threats to keep her from calling out his sleazy behaviour, or else.

*

Gem sat down in the reception area of the counselling office, waiting for her psyche crutch. Once again, it was a different room, up and another flight of stairs and into the eaves, where the Velux window overlooked the city's rooftops.

"Sorry about the climb – we just have to take what's available on the day," Angela said.

Being occupationally perceptive, Angela could sense another emotional barrage and so grabbed the tissue box that sat on the windowsill. The power of suggestion triggered a torrential outburst of weeping and wailing, and Gem apologised for losing her shit minutes into the session.

"My father, he never showed," Gem said.

"That's a shame," Angela said.

Despite the bout of self-pity and regret that followed her home, she was able to talk to Elis, whose completely honest and empathetic reaction to her plight brought her back down to earth.

"How do you shake the bitter disappointment?" Gem said. "Maybe I need hypnotherapy, not counselling."

"Elis?" Angela said.

"He's my partner."

"It's wonderful that you were able to tell him how you feel."

The cornerstone moment made Gem realise that she didn't need to suffer alone any more, and, of course, a problem shared, etc. Also, there was really no point in worrying about the actions of others; one might as well kick against concrete. The aim of counselling was to help guide Gem through a dark tunnel and into a world of relative tranquillity, but with no guarantee of a seamless journey.

The closing subject was group therapy, or sitting in a circle and talking to other like-minded people who had been through similar trauma. Gem had a cynical view of such gatherings, thinking they were just chatty forums for attention-seekers rather than an opportunity to seek solace and common ground. It just wasn't her bag of goodness, and she agreed to carry on as before: 'one to one', albeit with an open mind.

*

A glass of red was welcome nectar, and Gem made no apology for downing it in a few eager gulps. She had forgotten about the diamond-encrusted skull pendant that was laid on the lounge table.

"It fell out of the bathroom cabinet," Elis said.

"I can't remember putting it there."

"I take it it's not yours," Elis said.

"No, it belonged to a guy I used to work with," she said.

"Oh yeah?" Elis said, winking.

This was life's way of eking out yet another ruinous tale, the regurgitation of which was going to drag her backwards through the vilest trauma once more.

"This won't be easy, so fill her up," Gem said, pointing to the wine glass.

Creepy Mark from Cork and Hammond was a full-on predator, from the numerous side swipes to one particular physical intrusion in the office kitchen. Describing the attack was gut-wrenching, especially as it all happened yards from where they were sat.

"I managed to stop him raping me, but the punches that followed knocked me sideways."

"Jenny did mention something about you being in hospital. Please tell me that the fucker is locked away in some prison cell right now."

"Yes, thanks to a witness who saw him leaving the flat, covered in blood," she said.

Elis sat for a moment, fighting his anger. Such was the harsh reality, there would always be men who believed it their God-given right to violate women – and Mark was one such toe rag.

*

Rache was clearing tables when Gem walked through to the café.

"The phone's been ringin' for you – some bloke called Malc," she said.

That ship had long since sailed, or so Gem thought, her expectations quashed by the passage of time.

"That's my father – he was supposed to meet me here

ages ago and never turned up," Gem said.

As they were talking, the white-suited man peered over his newspaper. It could have been a subconscious call for guidance, but the mutual stare erased Gem's bumbling hesitancy as if it were a passing rain cloud. She made a mental note to ring Malc and arrange one more meeting - the final chance for reconciliation.

*

The flat's renovations were almost complete, thanks to Elis, who had been making up for time lost due to illness. The owner now wanted it sold as soon as possible, so the rush was on to seek out alternative accommodation. Gem felt bad about being unable to attend all arranged viewings due to her working hours, even though Elis had a pretty good idea of location and which properties would suit.

*

Riding in the front passenger seat of Elis's old Ford transit was a little bumpy, though marginally better than a stuffy commuter train. The van had seen better days, and despite Elis's meagre attempt at tidying the interior, used paper cups and sandwich wrappers still festered in door pockets. They were en route to his grandparents' house in North London, and Gem had no idea what to expect or if they would even like her.

"Be warned – they're a little full-on," Elis sniggered.

An embracing welcome greeted the couple as they stepped through Pat and Graham's door – coats off, kettle on, and tactility personified. Gem had nil experience of genuine family get-togethers and how to behave around those who make considerable fuss.

"Go and make yourself comfy in the dining room," Pat said.

The table was generously laden, as if the whole street were coming for dinner, judging by the size of the home-baked meat pie in the centre, flourished with pastry leaves.

"I should have brought a doggy bag," Gem said, laughing.

The décor was very chintzy and covered in trinkets and mementoes, including a photograph of Elis as a young lad on the mantelpiece. An old teddy bear lay next to a box of toys tucked behind a slightly misplaced armchair.

"Go on, help yourself," Graham said, ladle-deep in mashed spud.

"It's so nice to finally meet you," Pat said, patting Gem's hand.

Aside from a perpetual dread of awkward questions when meeting new people – "Where are you from?", "What do your parents do for a living?", "Any siblings?", etc. – Gem was holding it together. Her past was not for open discussion, and the very thought of her mother induced bile. All that mattered was the 'here and now'.

Mid-way through the main course, Pat left his chair to fetch a bottle of wine and a corkscrew.

"We have a lot to discuss," she said.

Elis was handed a paper folder, with no idea of its contents.

"What's this?" he said.

"Open it," Pat said.

He was only sixteen years old when his father left for Dubai, leaving a policy with Pat and Graham for them to oversee until such a time that he needed money to make a substantial purchase, such as property. Judging by Elis's bewildered expression, the news had been totally unexpected, and he was consequently lost for words. Gem couldn't resist a crafty peek at the accompanying letter from his father, where there was mention of a child called Joseph – which would maybe explain the toys in the lounge. She inadvertently pointed to the name while glancing at Elis, wearing a 'what the fuck?' expression. Trust was a big deal in Gem's world, and this bore all the hallmarks of a family secret trying to force its way out of the family closet.

"What do I do now?" Elis said.

"Take it with you, and when you're ready, sign and post out the acceptance form," Pat said.

*

The journey home was awkward, as Gem battled with varying emotions. She wanted to know everything about Elis, including any history, shady or otherwise. Anything was better than finding out inadvertently.

"So, tell me about 'Joseph'?" she said.

"Please love, don't be mad. I was eighteen and at some party with this girl. We started fumbling around and one thing led to another. Next thing, I found out she was pregnant."

"I don't care – you should have told me," she said.

Later that evening, Elis opened up about how the news affected his life at such an early age. His father had always insisted he do the right thing and pay towards Joseph's upbringing, which would explain the addendum letter, outlining his son's share of the lump sum. Keeping up with regular child maintenance payments became a struggle, as did arranging visits with Joseph's mother, as she was never home and rarely answered his phone messages unless it was about money.

"Did you feel anything for her?" Gem said.

"No, it was just me being a lad – a few lagers and I would have shagged anybody."

Elis said, "And so I paid the price."

"I get it – I was no different."

"What do you mean?"

"I had sex with some guy back in Lanebridge, and we didn't use a condom."

"It's just too embarrassing when you're young."

"Yep, and so damned irresponsible."

Gem was in no way ready for kids, but felt duty-bound to suggest Elis fight for partial custody once they were settled into their own place.

*

The managerial tactics at Pineapple Indigo had distinctly changed since Gem's design success, and the pressure was on for her to repeat the process. Theo was on her case as soon as she removed her coat, barking deadlines and timeframes, while she soaked up the crap like a proverbial sponge.

"I am doing my best," she said to his wagging finger.

"Then try harder – the more rowers, the faster the boat," he said.

She was then expected to work even longer hours, and without extra pay, to keep things even. Enthusiasm for the role helped soothe the tension, but it wouldn't be long before that bridge began to buckle under the strain.

*

Gem climbed the stairs to the flat and immediately noticed that the door was ajar and the lock had been broken, leaving splintered wood shards scattered on the floor. She nervously stepped inside, should anyone be hiding, even though one could check every room with a single head-spin. The intrusion naturally triggered memories of the attack, and as she turned on the nearest light was met with a dismal scene: papers strewn, clothes on the carpet and every drawer and cupboard gaping open.

The police came to take the usual statement and to sweep the place for fingerprints, and all that seemed to be missing was the diamond-encrusted pendant that had been left on the lounge table. The female constable found a false nail lying on the rug by the sofa, and Gem reluctantly thought of Fran, who was last seen in dire straits and heading for the nearest refuge. She would have only been allowed to stay for one week before it was back to black.

Elis returned from an apartment viewing to find a

locksmith chiselling through the keyhole.

"As you can see, we've had a visitor – thankfully they only took the necklace," Gem said.

"Christ, are you sure – I left some cash on the dresser?"

Gem hadn't thought to check the bedroom, or even the drawer where the remainder of Hattie's stash was kept, but when she did, found the money gone. The woman was a seasoned thief who knew where to look, and it mattered not that she was ransacking her own sister's property.

The police left the flat, having covered all angles possible at that time. They headed for the hostel to query when Fran had vacated her room and to see if there were any clues as to where she might have gone.

The burglary was a wake-up call for Jenny as there had never been any functioning alarm as security for either the café or the flat above, which could seriously deter interest in the property. There were clearly far greater priorities than titivating the café's appearance, and, as a manager, this had simply been overlooked.

*

Theo had become a proverbial sticky thorn in Gem's side, snagging her skin and skewing her mental state. She was called into his office for a routine nit-pick, and while she understood the necessity to produce work quickly and efficiently, he couldn't seem to differentiate between human and robot.

His office was a clean-lined, 'state of the art' man-pad

which occupied most of the second floor. Gem sat down on the bright yellow sofa, the view from which overlooked the City of London through a sea of glass.

"How are things?" he said, his condescending ass perched on the curved desk.

"Okay, if I can just get on with it," Gem said, with a barbed tone.

"Word has it that you are having some sort of psychotherapy."

The intrusive statement struck several chords, the first one being that she had told no one in the workplace about the counselling – and so, which deceitful 'little bird' had breached confidentiality?

"Please correct me if I'm wrong, but I'm not legally required to discuss matters of a personal nature."

"Unless it affects your productivity, and then it's entirely my business."

Gem was repulsed by such a blatant attempt to manipulate her with ill-gotten information.

"There is nothing in my contract to suggest this – you should maybe read up," Gem said.

The imposing sideswipe was totally unexpected. Theo had defaced the rule book, plunging to seedy depths and eroding what little trust she had in the man.

*

The following morning, Gem called her union rep and unearthed some considerable shenanigans. It turned out there was no case to question the work performance of anyone having therapy, at least without a thorough investigation. The chink in the armour was her meagre probationary period – she could either sit it out and risk further violation or make moves to get the fuck out from under Theo's manky coat-tails.

Using her phone was a knee-jerk reminder to also ring her father, reinforced by the white-suited man's weird interaction. She dialled the number once again, with a racing heart, half hoping he wouldn't answer.

"Hey, thanks for calling back," he said, breathless, like he had crawled to the phone through a wind tunnel.

"So, where were you before?" she said.

"I got off at the wrong station."

"You should have called me – I could have hung on."

As his hesitation duly confirmed, there really was no excuse, and therefore she didn't matter that much. Just another passing ship: "Oh, look – there she goes, *again*."

"You know where I live, so call in at the café – and if I'm in, we can talk. I'll leave it there."

The soulless, noncommittal conversation in an attempt to stir the man's vacuous soul was terminated. As she placed her phone back inside her bag she disturbed the piece of paper on which she had initially written Malc's address. She took it out to read it again, over and over, the elusiveness of the man gnawing at her insides. It was the weekend, and Elis was working extra hours, so Gem decided to take a South West train to Malc's house in Surrey. All she wanted was to meet and have a civilised conversation.

The taxi pulled up outside a modest detached house

with an elaborate front garden, and the vintage Jag that supposedly belonged to a friend sat on the driveway. As she stepped out of the cab, saw a blonde-haired woman standing in the large downstairs window. It was hard to conceive of this new distraction, and there was no telling what would happen if Gem knocked on the door to introduce herself in a world where she may not technically exist. Rather than turn back, she decided to play detective and discreetly hang around, like a regular nosy parker. There was a partly concealed view of the back garden, where she could see Malc and the woman flitting around. It was all very cosy-normal as the couple rummaged in the garden shed for the sun loungers, rubbing against each other in the process. The scene reflected a side of her father that she had never seen, and the total opposite to how it was during her childhood years, living in perpetual sadness with the Lanebridge monster.

Gem finally made her way home, pondering the bigger picture, having previously imagined Malc as a loner, whose diabolical marriage had changed his view of women. Truth was, she didn't know him at all, and he had made damn sure of that.

*

Following countless unremarkable viewings, Gem and Elis had finally found a two-bedroomed ground-floor apartment approximately five miles from the café, and they were off to visit the vacant property, to assess furniture and décor requirements prior to moving in. It was weird to be pulling into an allocated parking space directly outside, and Gem felt the magnetic pull of the place, almost like she had been there before.

"This is definitely 'home,'" she said, standing in the middle of an empty lounge, envisaging the possible layout and colour schemes. Lost in the countless possibilities, a wiry distraction shimmied down from the ceiling light.

"Jesus fucking Christ," she said, leaping back.

The spider swung back and forth before landing in her hair, with what felt like the tiniest of fingers tickling the roots. She leaned forward to shake her head, and the damned thing fell out and onto the floor. It didn't look normal: mechanical, almost, cracking and hissing as it writhed around on the carpet. Once aligned, it manoeuvred its way towards the skirting board.

"You okay?" Elis said, peering around the kitchen door.

"Come and check this guy out," she said, pointing to the black mass.

"What you talking about?" he said.

"The spider, look," she said, pointing.

He just laughed. "Have you been smoking Fran's ganja?"

*

The staffroom was a veritable gossip box of competitive whispers that made Gem's teeth itch, and she would not have been there had there been somewhere other than her desk to eat lunch. Two female colleagues were chatting in the seated area, reminiscent of kids in the school playground, sharing insults and sniggering at fellow pupils. It was probably equally as childish for Gem to then pretend to close the door so they would assume she had left.

"I should have got that job, fucking bitch," said woman A to woman B, mimicking the 'thanks, but no thanks' rejection speech: "'Thank you, Miss Raven, for your application …'"

"Is she still seeing your mother?" said woman B.

Gem balked at the bitter exchange of disparaging words, which now made perfect sense. As Angela's surname was Raven, she knew for certain who had been spilling way too many beans.

Chapter 8

A regular charity event was underway at the café, promoted by Gem and her nifty artwork that was plastered all over the café walls, shared on social media and posted through nearby mailboxes. Local volunteers had brought in pastries and cakes to make extra money for a chosen cause, so it was all hands on deck, serving a regular stream of customers. Sure enough, the white-suited man had been there since the start, securing his usual seat in the corner.

Rache was a little subdued, ploughing on without any interaction. She had been holding out for promotion – that is, until Jenny started interviewing for more staff without any mention, when she sensed that some young thing was about to fill the position of head waitress.

"Why don't you speak with Jenny?" Gem said.

"Nah, you know me. I ain't beggin'," Rache said, handing Gem a business card that was left by some guy yesterday. "Impressed wiv those posters, he was."

"Wow, I wasn't expecting anyone to notice," Gem said.

*

Dinner was waiting as Gem kicked off her shoes in the doorway. Elis was her saving grace amid a multitude of life's dysfunctional elements: an estranged father, thieving sister and a snidey boss. With one glance, he could sense whatever emotion lay beneath her delicate layers and that she longed to be in a better place both mentally and physically.

"I went to Malc's house the other day," she said.

"I don't know why you bother – he needs a kick up the jacksie," Elis said.

"I didn't, really – there was another woman."

"What, like, they were together?"

"Oh, yes – they were together all right. Anyway, I came away, I felt sick."

*

Gem took out the business card from the front pocket of her apron before throwing it into the laundry basket. The layout was concise and professional: 'Longview Designs – Commercial Advertising'. She rang Adrian, whose number was stated on the reverse, and introduced herself as the poster girl from Clipper Café. He went on to explain the search for a graphic artist who could produce eye-catching logos and images for companies in the food industry, such as takeaways, coffee outlets and restaurant chains. It sounded like an interesting and challenging opportunity, and so a meeting was arranged to discuss a possible role. The thought of leaving Pineapple Indigo was disappointing, and she felt that the company had failed her in so many ways. Young blood should be valued, not disrespected by the power-hungry. The so-called sisterhood was also a big red flag for men who valued tits and ass above ability.

*

A particularly challenging counselling session was a door's width away, and Gem was poised and ready to share details of the staffroom eavesdrop. Even the regular niceties were brittle, with no way of moving forward until the breach had been acknowledged.

"Does your daughter work for Pineapple Indigo?" Gem said.

"Yes, she's more on the distribution side."

"It's just that I overheard a conversation between two women at work – one talking about having failed to 'get the job' and slagging off the successful candidate, which was me. The other woman then asked, in her words, 'Is she still seeing your mother?'"

Angela's brain was whirring, as she tried to establish how her daughter could have been privy to Gem's therapy – unless the girl had been sifting through her mother's diary. Gem then went on to say that her boss was now using the information to manipulate her position, forcing her to look for another job.

"I am so sorry, Gem – I will sort this."

"I do hope she is aware of the potential damage to your reputation."

The cringeworthy statement seemed a little too heavy, in hindsight, as Gem's intention wasn't to rub salt into the wound. Angela offered Gem the chance of seeing another counsellor in the interim, but weeks of therapy could not simply be rewound like some old cassette tape, and thoughts of repeating her childhood sagas to a complete stranger was unpalatable.

*

A moving date had been set, and Gem was looking forward to a new beginning and sharing domestic life with her man. There was still the conundrum of whether she should keep on with the occasional shift at the café or call time on what would be more of an obligation than an actual job. Money wasn't a mitigating factor any more, just the friendships she had made while working there.

*

It was the morning of her interview with Adrian, and Gem stepped off the over-ground train towards Longview Advertising. She had researched the company, which was a far cry from Pineapple Indigo and more a basic setup on the outskirts of the city. There were only a handful of employees, and it seemed much more suited to a girl whose social etiquette wasn't a strong point. Above all else, she wanted to be valued as a talented artist and not just some 'college sprout'. The corporate workhouse had been an interesting experience, with endless interns passing through a tightly packed organisation, like a people conveyor belt, with no room for weakness or hesitation in the creative bullring.

Adrian gave a brief outline of what Longview Advertising was all about and a vocal inventory of some impressive contracts, some with recognisable brand names. The suitable candidate would work regular hours, with the occasional call for overtime, as required, in return for a decent salary and a private pension. Initiative and instinctive ability were high on the agenda, with an expectation to create impressive designs, sometimes with only a rough spec. It sounded perfect, and her desire to do it justice would dominate all else, at least until she found her feet. Adrian knew she was already working for a prestigious art and design company, and so was naturally curious as to why she came forward. Gem kept it simple: she was searching for employment in a quieter hub rather than a large central location, and with the hope of being more appreciated. As managers roll, he wasn't an archetypical stiff suit, but rather a much more down-to-earth, approachable guy.

"I just want to prove my worth without having to fight like a prize cock for recognition," she said.

"I totally get that – there are no egos here," he said.

He skimmed through her portfolio with an expression of reassurance, and therefore didn't interrogate each piece ad nauseam.

"I just have a few other candidates to see, but will have hopefully made my decision by later today."

Gem stood from her chair, shook Adrian's hand and thanked him for the meeting. She made her way back to the train station, trying not to overthink, as there was really no point. Finding a job had so far been pretty easy, having clinched the Pineapple Indigo job while she was still in college, so it was best left to chance rather than blind expectation.

*

Cappuccino with extra sprinkles awaited Gem as she arrived at the café for an impromptu shift. The white-suited man had just left, his newspaper still open on the table and a spider's corpse sprawling the bottom of his empty cup. It was hard to imagine that it had just crawled in, then drowned in the few drops of coffee that were left, especially as the spider sightings were growing more and more frequent. She had been reading some psychology book and about certain objects and their spiritual interpretations – like pennies, feathers, pins etc. – and wondered if such creatures carried a similar subliminal message.

*

Elis was dozing on the sofa and Gem was tiptoeing around the place, trying not to wake him. Dizzy spells had been driving him nuts and, sometimes, resting was the only way to stop the room from spinning.

"Hey girl, come here," he said, with one eye open.

"I should call the doctor, you know," she said.

"I'm fine. Anyway, how was the interview?"

"Not heard anything, so we'll see," she said.

There was a time when she had no one to worry about, but now her caring instincts were fully charged, and she had even considered staying home the following day so that he wouldn't be in the flat alone. Babying the man wasn't part of the relationship deal, and, as he reiterated time and again, partners were not parent substitutes.

*

That moment when you wake up and the thought of work fills you with dread is no walk in the park. Elis was propped against his pillow, watching her get dressed and denying the lethargy of a sleepless night. He had barely mentioned the move, and Gem was already over-thinking, having sensed his worry of becoming unwell

141

and having to push back the date. Anyway, she was perfectly capable of lifting and shifting without any assistance, communicated through her stubborn, non-negotiable stance. With that, she left the bedroom to make coffee, praying that a more productive and pleasurable alternative was about to clip the horizon.

Gem was met with various assigned projects as she stepped into the office, swamping her from the get-go. There was always time to indulge in wicked thoughts: *Fuck Theo and his workhouse rule, just get your stuff and go.*

As she hung her coat on the back of the door, Theo was already in the corner, sneering at the view that was in no way comparable to his own office window's landscape sprawl. The man was like a shop mannequin, all iron-pressed in polished leather shoes with evenly tied laces.

"Can I help you?" she said, hoping the half-measured attempt to gratify his presence would slice through the pointless convo.

"I've been thinking, we should start over – I was out of line before," he said, pressing his groin against the storage cupboard.

"Done," she said, sensing a flirtatious switch. "But I really do need to crack on – deadlines and all."

"Sure," he said, with an unmistakable pervy glare, slamming her into the wall with a piston thrust.

Sex was now the power-grab, some last-ditch attempt to tease out Gem's loyalty – an office screw to keep a job that was already hers. There were some who would plunge to seedy depths to secure their position, but *she* would rather chew her arms off than get jiggy with the corporate toad. She was so done with testosterone trials, of the profession's high flyers, each with the same twisted objective.

*

Elis's hobnailed boots were still by the door, next to toolbox, along with other handyman paraphernalia. Gem found him in the bedroom, trying to put on his slippers and cursing at each failed attempt.

"I can hardly move," he said. "The phone's been ringing, but I just couldn't …"

"It's fine, really," Gem said, trying to appease his broken and bereft 'dying bird' spirit.

"No, it's not – it could have been Adrian calling about the job."

Ever stoical, he managed to limp into the lounge with the aid of the walking stick he had vowed to throw in the trash, as if the useless tube of stainless steel metal somehow defined his physical status.

Gem rang Adrian anyway, as she was all out of waiting with bated breath. He apologised for not getting back sooner and promptly offered her the position, which was just as well as she was about to jack Pineapple Indigo and its petty chauvinism. The news brought pure, unadulterated joy, a fanfare of trumpets blowing fast and hard. She was now fully determined to address the confidentiality breach prior to resignation, shopping corporate git Theo and 'gobshite' Selina, who had both played a significant part in forcing her out. At least then she could leave with her head held high.

*

Coursework and unpredictable train times were binding as Gem yearned to sink her teeth into the new job, especially as the company had just taken on a lucrative contract for some major restaurant chain. There was no pressure from anyone, and yet she was breathing down her own neck, echoes of constant surveillance still reverberating, like a little 'Theo' doll dangling before her.

The enforced break in routine counselling sessions had been far from ideal, as Gem had grown steadily reliant on the emotional prop to help battle her inner demons, like persistent flecks of dirt floating in white paint – small, but distinct. The investigation into the confidentiality breach had resulted in the expulsion of Selina from Pineapple Indigo, much to Angela's embarrassment. There was no excuse for such abhorrent behaviour, dicing with reputations, and all because certain people had no decorum or the self-discipline to shut the fuck up when talking in a public domain. Gem would have preferred Selina's slack jaw on a spike, if only to satisfy an unresolved bitterness.

"I do hope we can move on from all this," Angela said.

"Yes, so do I," Gem said.

"Where were we, anyway?" Angela said, settling into the chair.

"A lot has happened since the last session – I now

144

have a new job and a new home," Gem said.

"Progress indeed."

"Like rolling through mud onto dry land."

"Is there any news from your father?"

That little skid mark on white linen stiffened Gem's spine, despite everything.

"I got the skankiest letter, asking me to ring him, so I did. We arranged to meet and he got on the train but missed the station. He called the café when I wasn't there, so I called and left a voicemail, inviting him to the flat. I was just sick of it, so I decided to visit his house and there was this woman," Gem said.

"And then what did you do?" Angela said.

"I hung around for a while, and they were all lovey-dovey in the back garden. I couldn't stay, you read me?" Gem said.

Angela suggested that she write one final letter, spilling all that she had intended to say at the meeting. It would be the final salute and could be posted or simply thrown in the trash. All this miscommunication was a total farce, and who was to say whether he actually read any of it.

"I'll think about it, but believe me, it won't be pretty," Gem said.

*

Elis was due a health check and Gem had taken time out to accompany him to the hospital. Waiting around for any kind of medical intervention was utterly draining, surrounded by crisp cotton uniforms and a bleached aroma. After an exhaustive wait, they were called into a consulting room where the doctor was reading Elis's notes on the computer screen. The trail began some two years ago, when he was diagnosed following a routine eye test and the optician referred him for further investigation. He knew something was wrong, with fatigue and general aches, especially after playing football for the local team. The lads would laugh because he didn't always see the ball and would continually miss training or feign injury, as a real one would have been debilitating.

"So, how is it going?" Dr Seaton said.

Elis didn't say a great deal, except to call out the latest relapse as being "inconvenient" and "irritating" etc., regardless of the symptoms. He had also been avoiding the general practitioners, fearing it may lead to a further course of steroids, which cause weight gain and other repugnant side effects.

"And how is your eyesight –any deterioration?"

"It's worse when I'm tired – the usual flickering and blurring."

The consultant invited Elis to lie on the paper-covered couch to examine his spine and joints, and to stare into each ear with a torch. Everything seemed fine, with no obvious changes, but he was still young and better able to withstand the trauma of intermittent attacks. The doctor suggested that stress may have triggered the latest episode, with organising the move and coordinating events before and after contributing. They finally left the medical room with a prescription for different medication and a further appointment date for a routine MRI scan in six months' time. Gem had learned a lot about the condition and therefore realised there was no need to smother Elis like some weird obsessive with Munchausen's by proxy.

Elis didn't fancy cooking and had ordered takeaway so they could dine while lounging on the sofa. He went to the kitchen to fetch a bottle of wine, and Gem heard chuntering, something about there being no glasses: "Aw, not teacups again", blah. She joined him to search through the many boxes, trying to read the labels, which were now a little blurry.

"There isn't room for both of us," she said, shooing him back to the lounge. "I'll bring them through."

The champagne flutes were in the last crate and as she took a towel to wipe them down she unearthed some wiry black legs where they had been standing. She carefully placed the glasses down on the kitchen worktop to gather composure, recalling the last encounter, which had scared her half to death. She peered into the crate to check if what she saw was actually real, and the thing leapt out and latched onto her face. Suddenly she was staring through a menagerie of black furry lines, gripping her head, writhing and squirming. She managed to claw it away and cast it across the room.

"Fucking hell, this can't be happening!" she said.

The creature lay twitching, a heap of threads and a tiny head that was oozing some sort of pus. Her love of spiders was fast abating, and the desire to gather up its broken body and place it in a safe place was no more. Instead, she used the dustpan to batter it senseless, swept it up and tipped it into the bin.

"You'll never believe what just happened ..." Gem said, walking back into the lounge, holding the required glasses.

Elis appeared to be hiding, emerging moments later wearing some cheeky bow tie and the craziest smile.

"Close your eyes and hold out your hand," he said.

"Yeah, right – come on, I hate surprises," she said.

A gold ring, clutching several diamonds within an open box, now sat on her palm.

"So, will you marry me?" he said.

And so the man's commitment was declared, contradicting the familiar internal derogatory groan of her mother's voice: "Who the fuck would want you?"

"Yes, yes, of course I will," she said, wrapping her arms around his neck.

Elis had made the purchase some weeks ago and had been waiting for the right time to ask. He then suggested a housewarming party to make it official, and so Gem began compiling a list of proposed guests, buffet food, tablecloths and napkins.

The apartment would need more furniture, including some borrowed chairs, a lick of paint, and to be clear of the many boxes that littered every room.

*

Adrian was attending a training course in Germany and

had left basic 'how to run the gaff' instructions in his absence, including an itinerary of expected phone calls, recommended responses and a link to a spreadsheet to log any paid invoices. He must have considered Gem's potential managerial capabilities, even though such a task was daunting for a relatively new employee. So much for an easy couple of weeks, she thought.

*

The housewarming invites had been duly posted and she was en route to the Clipper Café to deliver Rache and Jenny's personally. As per the new name tag, Rache was now 'assistant manager' and busy training a new waitress.

"See, you got the promotion after all?" Gem said.

"I know," Rache said, winking. "Anyway, meet Sally, who started yesterday."

It was now habitual to glance over and expect the white-suited man to be sitting in the corner, but apparently, he hadn't frequented the café for a while. Gem wondered why she would even care about someone with whom she had yet to exchange one word.

"Ah well, I hope you and Jenny can make it to the party," Gem said, placing two sealed envelopes on the counter.

"You shoulda brought one in for that sista of yours," Rache said, laughing. "Been lookin' for you, she 'as, boastin' abaat bein' back at work."

"Just tell her about it – she'll turn up if there's free wine."

Congrats to the woman who had seemingly managed

to miraculously turn things around, despite eviction and a vehement craving for those giant spliffs. Let her turn up and listen to Gem on the podium, boring her senseless with a detailed analogy of *her* own life successes.

*

The office was incredibly quiet, almost as if clients were holding out for Adrian's return. Gem took advantage of the free time to draft a concluding letter to her father, her brow creasing as she penned the mental autopsy. Once again, the painful sift through life's dirty laundry was a long overdue ricochet of seeping rawness, reaching for his blackened heart or whatever was keeping the blood flowing through those veins. She could only assume he was alive somewhere beyond, the direst apology for a human being.

*

The train was late and Gem was fiddling with her eyelashes, something she did when anxious or tired. The platform was packed with people repeatedly gazing at their mobile phones and the station clock, eager to make tracks. A fracas struck up among the lingering crowd, and Gem turned towards a woman who was shaking her daughter by the shoulders.

"You always do this! I should bloody well leave you here," she said.

"I don't want to go," the girl said, crying.

Gem had no real understanding of what was going on, nor was it any of her business, but the scene cut her to the bone, building an inner crescendo of emotion as the argument continued. The woman then pushed the girl to the floor amid gasps and pointing fingers, at which point Gem exploded like a freshly lit firework.

"You can't do that – she's just a child, for God's sake!" she said, helping the girl to her feet.

"You should mind your own business, bitch," the woman said.

"But there's no need for violence, none whatsoever," Gem said.

The noise alerted a nearby security guard who wandered over to investigate. Although he was oblivious to the unfolding drama, he immediately assumed that Gem was the instigator, some head case who was trying to cause trouble.

"You need to calm down, madam, or I will have to escort you from the station."

"So am I supposed to just stand and watch while this woman rags her daughter about in public?" Gem said.

"I don't see a problem here. Please, come with me," the guard said, marching her towards the nearest exit.

Gem replayed the chain of events over in her head to make doubly sure it wasn't just a simple misinterpretation, knowing her heightened sensitivity to perceived child abuse. She even fought with the desire to return to the station and challenge the woman further, which would have only dug a deeper hole. It was so incredibly hard to turn a blind eye to people who believe it to be their God-given right to hurt kids, just like her own mother. Even those who were meant to protect often ignored the abuser, because it was easier than challenging their behaviour.

*

Not a single accepting or declining invitation for the housewarming had been received, so Gem had no idea how many would be attending the party. Regardless, she had prepared a generous spread of sandwiches, salad and cold chicken, with pizza on baking trays waiting in a preheated oven.

"Where is everybody?" she said.

Ever-stoic Elis was lounging on the sofa, reading a newspaper. "Chill out, they'll be here."

An hour later, the first guests were knocking, and, typically, Rache and Jenny had brought an ample supply of wine and flowers.

"So good to see you," Gem said, inviting them in.

"You're lookin' great, babe," Rache said.

The framed sketches above the wooden cabinet caught Jenny's eye. "You've come a long way since then," she said.

"Get ready," Rache said, pointing through the window at Fran, who was teetering down the garden path in stiletto heels.

It was time for Gem to don a different persona, to pretend everything was just fine and dandy, and temporarily forget that Fran was likely responsible for the burglary, so as not to ruin her own soiree. With a painted-on smile, she welcomed her sister into the apartment, clutching a bottle gift bag flourished with the usual tacky ribbon – and orchids, always orchids.

Fran's drastic transformation turned a few heads – cropped short jet-black hair; a faux-leather mini-skirt kissing her arse crack; and a flimsy camisole with spindly straps to accentuate spray-tanned shoulders. The archetypical attention-grabbing garb was more nightclub chav than low-key party attire.

"Hey, sis, loving the new pad," she said, her glitzy eyes panning the room. Time had clearly erased her previous lapse into dishonest behaviour and was back on 'Mary Jane', and as high as a fucking kite.

Gem beckoned Elis into the lounge. "Say hello to my sister," she said.

"At last – I have heard *so* much about you," he said.

"All good, I hope, and you're just how I imagined – cutesy as fuck," she said, pinching his cheek.

It was pure gold to watch the unlikely interaction unfold: Elis and his penchant for filtering out bullshit, while nodding and smiling in all the right places.

It was midway through the evening and the apartment was a vibrant haven of wine-induced laughter, house music and slurry conversation. Elis had invited a few work friends and their wives, who were occupying the sofa and Graham and Pat's chair loans. The Clipper Café crowd were the only ones standing on the carpet, half-shuffling to the playlist.

Elis called for everyone to gather round, pulling Gem to his side before making a surprise announcement. He took the swanky ring from the little blue box and placed it on her finger, causing considerable blushing.

"You just know when you meet the right girl," he said.

"That's it, then – shackled for life," she said.

The crowd gave a rapturous applause and raised their glasses in the air to toast the lovebirds. Jenny and Rache stepped in to admire the ring, spouting the usual well-meaning gestures.

"Where has the princess gone?" Rache said, quizzing Fran's absence.

"God knows, but I best find her," Gem said.

The kitchen was empty, despite all the bottles of booze that were stacked like skittles along the work surface. Gem had looked everywhere but the bathroom where there was a distinct reek of ganja seeping up through the doorframe.

"You in there?" she said, knocking.

"Yeah, gimme a sec," Fran said, followed by an obligatory flush.

"Come on, we only have the one loo," Gem said.

The door opened slowly, in a vague attempt to stem the evidence, which then filled the hallway from top to bottom.

"You've been smoking that shit again," Gem said.

"Its fine – just one puff, that's all," Fran said, lying her tits off again.

"For Christ's sake – what is happening to you?" Gem said, backing Fran's weed-riddled ass against the wall. "It's never just *one* puff, or *one* useless relationship or *one* impulsive break-in to fund whatever gets you off, no matter what the fucking damage."

"I didn't hear you moaning when I stole from our *mother* – you snatched my hand off when I gave you a share," Fran said, clutching at wilting straws.

"That was different – I deserved every damn penny. But the café flat, goddamn it – please tell me it wasn't you that ransacked our bedroom for a necklace and a few lousy quid?"

"Go fuck yourself, *sis*," Fran said.

"Wait up, now I know why that guy came to see you before. That was no boyfriend – I bet he was a fucking drug dealer! What do you do now, meet one his shifty colleagues on a street corner?"

It made perfect sense, all of it. The bloke came looking for her at the Renaissance apartment, which was why Phil locked her out, so she then needed somewhere to hide, plus more cash to fund the habit and pay the ever-increasing debt. Gem was enraged, and even suspected the woman had been creeping around the new apartment before visiting the bathroom.

Fran ran out like her arse was a raging fire – rumbled, but not shamed. That would be impossible.

Elis wasn't the least bit surprised by the clash of heads. Fran was a lost connection, void of consideration and respect, and she would just keep coming back, like a heap of dust blowing in – expecting forgiveness, time and again.

"Your mother certainly has a lot to answer for," he said.

*

Gem was nursing the vilest hangover, as if her head was being pounded by an iron pan. Elis had eased off the wine and was already up and gathering empty bottles and paper buffet plates to shame her weak constitution. It had been the best party, if a little tainted by her sister's drug-induced malfunction.

A combination of guilt and the feeling as if something was lightly stroking her skin drove Gem out from under the duvet. She stood and tentatively turned to look at the mattress, where there was a sprawling black spider, its long spindly legs beyond all rational dimensions. If it hadn't been vaguely moving, it could have been mistaken for one of those creepy replicas plastered on glass during Halloween season.

"Where did you come from, damn it – the devil's outhouse?" she said.

The occurrences were becoming commonplace and purposeful, though for what reason was a total mystery. As the oversized critter began its descent to the floor, Gem rolled up a magazine and smashed it, dead. Its crumpled remains then slowly dissolved into a powder-like substance. Elis wandered in to find her naked, staring down at the black ash.

"You been walking around in your boots again? Look at the dirt," he said.

Gem brushed herself down and straightened the bed covers.

"Oh, my God, what about Polly?" she said, out of nowhere.

Most of the guests hadn't directly replied to the

housewarming invites, but Polly was a stickler for such things and always made the effort to accept or decline. Gem had also lost track of the pregnancy, and so was immediately thrust into the idea that something must be wrong.

"Elis, I need to be somewhere," she said.

"Okay – where?" he said.

My friend, Polly – she never got in touch about the party."

"So just give her ring," Elis said.

"I have, but she's not answering."

Gem pulled out a T-shirt from the gap in the top drawer and hopped into some socks on her way to the lounge.

*

The journey to Kensington in Elis's old van was typically slow, what with sluggish traffic, road works and hitting every possible traffic light. Gem tried to keep a lid on the catastrophising and stared out the window, counting dogs, people, houses, anything to distract her straying mind. Within yards of Polly's ground-floor flat, Gem could see that all the blinds were down and slats closed, and it was almost lunchtime. She knocked and waited on the step, beside a black-and-white cat that was looking as equally lost. Just as she was about give up, Polly's door opened very slightly.

"I thought you were some cold caller – you'd better come in," she said.

The living room was a salubrious scrapheap, with a sofa covered in dirty clothes and empty takeaway cartons on the designer coffee table. It could be postnatal chaos, except it just didn't feel right. Polly's bump had gone and there was no sign of a baby's presence – nappies, crib, bottles, etc.

"In case you're wondering, I lost it," Polly said, tears pooling her darkened eyes.

"Oh my God – I'm so sorry," Gem said.

"He was stillborn, at just twenty-eight weeks," Polly said.

"How's Teddy?"

"Dunno, he's gone to his parents' house."

Suffering the worst loss was enough, without being alone to battle the emotional pain. The guy should have been there, no excuses.

It was early on in the pregnancy so Polly just assumed she had caught a tummy bug, until the pain grew stronger and then intolerable. She was 'blue-lighted' to hospital, overwhelmed by anxiety about the baby and the prospect of an early labour.

"Get some things together – you can come and stay with us for a few days," Gem said.

"It's okay, I would rather be here," Polly said.

Whether it was Gem's intuition or a narrow assumption, Gem sensed that Polly wasn't being entirely honest and that Teddy had, in fact, moved out – period. When pressed, Polly revealed that she had found some dodgy text messages from other women on his mobile, dating back to well before she became pregnant.

"What will you do about the flat?" Gem said.

"I'm taking my sweet time – Teddy's parents can easily afford the rent, and it's not my fault that he's a cheating scumbag."

The cad was living proof that monetary embellishment and private school tutoring in no way guaranteed a sense of responsibility and moral intuition. Polly was right to play the game and squeeze every last drop of gratuity to help her through.

"You can tell me to mind my own, but what about your mum in all this?" Gem said.

"Remember Dave, the guy I told you about?"

"That's her new beau, right?"

"Well, now it's Connor – she loves men more than her kids."

"That's too bad."

"No, it's not, believe me."

Gem would have stayed much longer if Elis hadn't been patiently waiting outside, so they agreed to meet as soon as Polly was up to it mentally and physically. There were college courses and subsequent job opportunities to pursue, and Gem would be on hand to help, whenever needed.

*

The policy cheque had finally arrived through the post and was lying on the lounge table.

"What's this?" Gem said.

"Probably bad timing, but you may as well take a

look," Elis said, all wistful.

The princely sum of £30,000 was mega, as neither Gem nor Elis had had any concept of how much money was actually due.

"That's amazing! I'm so pleased for you," Gem said.

"It's ours, and, to use your words, non-negotiable," he said.

Acceptance of anything was a hard ask for Gem, especially as she had barely entered Elis's life – what right did she have? Granted, she had snatched Fran's hand off when it came to Hattie's stash, as minuscule compo for damage that was already done.

*

At the end of a two-day training course, Gem was on the train back to London. To kill time she tipped her bag onto the carriage table, and among the contents was a counselling appointment card for a date that had long since expired. The subliminal message gave her the chance to elongate the gap between sessions and test her resolve, but instead, she caved in and dialled Angela's number and left a voicemail to rearrange 'just' one more appointment. It was a destructive loop in her assumption that talking further lessened the chance of a meltdown.

*

Elis had been waiting until she arrived home to warm dinner, so that they could eat together.

"I saw some old guy hanging round the gate when I got back," he said.

"Ah, probably flogging a new roof or some other

overpriced renovation."

"Dunno – he scarpered as soon as the van pulled up."

They were like an old married couple, talking through their day with coffee cups on 'his and hers' coasters on the lounge table. Elis was like a calming pill, bending and twisting like a sail in the wind.

"I talked to Joseph today," he said. "He's dying to see the new apartment, so I invited him for tea tomorrow."

"Of course, I can't wait to meet him," Gem said.

Children had never really figured in Gem's life until now, and she really didn't have the foggiest idea of how to *be*, whether he was the brat who stomped his feet if there was no ketchup, or a perfect little boy with manners and consideration. She could do with an 'idiot's guide' to help with a considerable list of fundamental questions – what to play, say and do to keep the child sweet.

*

Thank-you cards gave Gem the perfect excuse for an impromptu stop-off at the Clipper Café. The frontage was now hidden behind scaffolding to facilitate repointing of brickwork, an exterior paint job and frosted logo embellishment to enhance the main window.

"You're getting all spruced up, I see," Gem said.

"And Jenny's taking over the tenancy," Rache said. "Talkin' o' changes, the white-suited geezer asked abaat you the ova day."

"Really – go on, what did he sound like?"

"Like im from that song, 'Frilla', yeah, that's the one."

It was just how Gem had imagined, some old bard

with a dark, grainy voice, all moody and mysterious. She wished she had been there, if only to satisfy her curiosity.

*

The drop-leaf table was now central and away from the wall, so it could be fully extended to facilitate an extra place setting. Gem went to answer the door where Joseph and his mother were stood beneath the overhang, sheltering from a heavy shower.

"Come on in, I didn't know it was raining," she said.

The lad was dithering behind his mother's coat-tails, hiding from Gem like she was the weird lady on the bus, offering boiled sweeties to complete strangers. Beth apologised for him being so painfully shy, which was preferable to the lad tearing round the house, unleashed. Elis emerged from the kitchen and, as if by magic, neutralised Joseph's fearful disposition.

"Come on – let's go check on the pie," he said, taking his hand.

The women stood silently in the lounge, each searching for something to say, having never met before.

"Does he like school?" Gem said.

"Sort of, but he struggles with routine and discipline," Beth said.

A recent autism diagnosis made sense of Joseph's mind-set and behaviour akin to a child much younger than his eight years. Beth had been haggling with school governors to secure one-to-one tutoring as opposed to the alternative: attending a special needs school miles from home. Elis had made no mention of the condition, but must have been quietly reading up, judging by the fresh titles on the bookshelf, covering child psychology and Asperger's.

"I'll leave you to it, then," Beth said, taking an opportune moment to leave while Joseph was out of the room.

"Elis has my number if there are any problems."

"I'm sure everything will be fine," Gem said.

The atmosphere was a little tense as Gem dithered over dinner plates, feeling overly clumsy. Joseph watched intently as she served the food, and then proceeded to scoff with abandon, nodding his head as if to gratify each succulent mouthful. Elis tried not to react and just smiled at Gem from across the table.

Apparently, autistic children's expressions were often nondescript, so Gem struggled to interpret how Joseph was feeling, happy or sad. Regardless of the condition, discipline was still paramount, and Elis insisted that there was no pudding until everyone had finished the first course, no matter how many mini-tantrums.

"So what books do you like?" Gem said, plucking a question from mid-air while Elis fetched the dishes.

Joseph then leapt from his chair to go and rummage through his rucksack, returning to the table with a giant book of dinosaurs, parting the pages and hypnotised by the beasts within. Gem was 'wowing' and 'oohing', watching his expression while reciting each of their names and thinking she wasn't so bad after all and that being overly analytical was a waste of energy. Joseph sat out the next couple of hours on the sofa, wedged between Gem and Elis, watching nature programmes and drinking orange soda – a life less ordinary.

*

Gem watched from the window as Joseph climbed into Elis's van for the journey home. Once gone, she noticed a dark figure yards from the apartment. As it moved further down the pathway, the blur became clear vision of Malc, wearing a smart suit, all spruced up as if he had planned the occasion. His sudden and unexpected appearance was a shock, and she paused for several deep, therapeutic breaths before making a move.

"How did you find me?" she said, opening the door.

"Some lady at the Clipper Café gave me your new address."

He looked confused as to whom he was actually talking – a far cry from the willowy scrap of a girl with knotted hair and pasty skin. Finally seeing the man face to face failed to stir the vaguest emotion, having recently discovered that he was living his best life with some woman in a relatively posh area of London. The karma bus 'payback' for his blatancy during rare visits to *that house*, despite her very obvious physical deterioration, had reached fruition. If ever there was a non-saviour during those darkened days it was Malc, leaving Gem crippled by Hattie's heartlessness.

"I take it you got my letter," she said.

"Oh, yes – I certainly did," he said, pulling a crumpled piece of paper from his jacket pocket.

"Have you read it?"

"Of course and I … I get it."

"Get what?"

"That you're angry."

"Well, yes, just a little."

Pause.

"Why did you steal Hattie's money?"

The distinct jump was illogical, bypassing all the shittiest shit she had ever written, the deepest and darkest pain imaginable. Still, 'blacksheep' took the rap for everything, including Fran's thievery, and here she was, still padding the defence podium.

"I didn't, but she damn well knows who did … and so do you."

Not a scrap of sense came from the man's delusional ramblings, and sensing her disengagement the tone shifted to one of reflection, and with the merest shuffle towards the sofa's edge, Malc looked at her square on, his mouth gaping. It was as if he was on 'pause', to prevent whatever the fuck else he could blurt out that would ignite the embers.

"Thing is, I'm not your real father," he said.

Gem openly stared, replaying the words over in her head.

"What? So who is?" she said.

Following a hefty nose blow into the scabbiest of handkerchiefs, he talked of one unfortunate day when a work colleague called at the house and Hattie was alone. He forced his way in, raped her and beat her senseless, and when Malc returned home she was unconscious on the kitchen floor with her face covered in blood. The violent and annihilating intrusion turned their marriage upside down – and then Hattie discovered she was pregnant. He knew the child wasn't his but continued to deny the elephant in the room until some four years later, when he took a few strands from Gem's hairbrush to request a DNA test from the hospital. When the results came back, he told Hattie, who completely lost her shit and was unable to rationalise or contemplate living in the same way ever again.

"I just couldn't reach her."

"So that's why she hates me."

"And just about everyone else after that."

"But she was still my mother, right? What happened to all the love?"

And then Malc just abandoned ship, leaving Gem to the mercy of a disgruntled, bitter woman for whom Gem became a punch bag to get even.

To reject an innocent and dependent child, for any reason whatsoever, was totally unacceptable. Gem had been happy and thriving and part of a relatively normal family up until that point, and Malc's sinister backstory seemed to evoke genuine anguish and pain – too little, too late. He had chosen to serve himself above all else, using the opportunity to cut all responsible ties. Shame it had taken until now to call it out.

"So what happened to the rapist? Did he get sent down?"

"Hattie wouldn't even speak about it, so it was never reported."

"But he was on your payroll, for Christ's sake – did you just let him walk?"

What was worse: –a rapist for a father, or one who was perfectly happy to let a violent assault go unpunished, all because Hattie couldn't face an uncomfortable ricochet?

"I know, I'm pathetic, and I should have told you."

"Too damned right you should."

"So, who's the woman?"

"How do you know about her?"

"I came to the house and watched you from the street, just like you,"

Malc stuttered and writhed as he described a longstanding relationship with 'Carrie', stretching back to the violent argument with Hattie that Gem had witnessed as a child. He had been living a double life, hence the much more endearing distraction and awkward pretence whenever he came home.

"How did you meet her?" Gem said.

"She was a work colleague," Malc said.

"So, she would know the rapist?"

"Kind of."

Before the so called bitter truths could wreak any more damage, Gem drew a close to the very harsh and deeply wounding conversation. She watched as he disappeared through the garden gate and back to wilderness.

*

Gem was mentally fractured by the almighty bombshell and minutes away from falling to her knees when Elis's rickety white van pulled into the driveway. Pre-meltdown, she sat down on the sofa and opened a magazine to hold up to her crumpled face, thinking she could hide from the one person who was sure to see straight through the façade.

"Hey, girl, I didn't know you could read upside down," he said.

"Damn it," she said, feeling foolish. "That man who's been hanging around the apartment, well, it was Malc. He came back just after you left to take Joseph home," she said.

"That's your father, right?" he said.

"Well, no. Apparently, my *father* is some bloke from his workplace who raped my mother."

Elis sat down beside her, lost for words. Some people discover that they were adopted later in life, as babies or even young children, but to be born as a result of an abhorrent crime is in an entirely different league and off-the-scale soul-crushing. It was now abundantly clear why Malc was barely around during her early years, and carrying on with some sordid affair as a result. The humiliating memory of when Gem used to sit by his side, begging for attention like some old dog, now knowing that his mind was elsewhere, repulsed by the entrails of another man's lust. Turning up for her sixteenth birthday was the snagging point; the merest tread into father-daughter territory was a garbage attempt at rebuilding their friendship.

*

Sick days were a 'no-no' for an employee who eager to stay in the good books, but Gem was utterly miserable, trying to mend her wilting heart. The letter sent to Malc had upturned a monumental stone, and the deal was that she must now bury her past. It was the ultimate self-destruction, to be defined by the immoral actions and inscrutable behaviour of those who are meant to care.

*

With weekend bags packed and a tank full of petrol, Elis and Gem headed out for a weekend break away from home, and to hell with the straining coffers, having sunk all of their money into the new apartment. Jenny knew someone who had a cottage near the Kent coast and managed to get the couple a cheap deal for a few stolen days. Gem longed to breathe in and out without mental disorientation, to drink wine with abandon and spend quality time with the only man who could save her.

The cottage was off the beaten track and set within a wealth of trees, where the only audible traces of life were flowing water and birdsong – nature's paradise. Gem stepped out of the van to take in the woodland view where she would have happily pitched out until the coolness of dusk drove them back inside.

The holiday couple bobbed down beneath the tiniest doorframe and into a rustic kitchen where iron pans hung above an old Aga oven, like a feature spread from a *Country Living* mag. There was a vase of fresh flowers on the table and a welcome note on the French dresser.

"Would you just look at this place?" she said.

"Yep, it's beautiful, just like you," he said.

The man was full of shit like that and, in a fit of

giggles, gave chase towards the bedroom with Gem tagging behind, undoing her jeans. Intimacy was the ultimate repair kit, easily neglected during any kind of emotional turbulence.

Dinner was a conveniently pre-prepared salad, olives, pasta and wine, served with a flickering candle on an outside table, overlooking a garden full of scent and blossom. They sat for hours and well into the evening, evading previous traumas like nothing had ever happened – a harmonious interlude.

"I've been thinking," Elis said.

"Steady," Gem said, laughing.

"I want to start my own business."

He had been busy noting down all the details to prepare for an arranging meeting with the bank manager – cost of business rent, equipment, potential staff needs, etc., all waiting to be discussed.

"Sounds great, apart from all the stress that goes with it."

"It's just the beginning, love, lots to learn and prepare, including a logo when you're ready"

To have never experienced the sea or felt the sand between one's toes is rare for a young woman – sunlight glistening on endless water ripples, a sky full of gulls circling the rocks, the salty breeze, etc. There had never been a holiday or daytrip anywhere, or even a family walk to the local park to punctuate endless days filled with human ugliness.

*

Children were playing nearby, and one little boy was edging close to the waves. Once again, Gem found herself scanning the beach to look for Mum or Dad, even though it was not her responsibility to even consider what may or may not happen.

"Calm down love, it's nothing to do with us," Elis said.

"But what if he can't swim?"

A man was shouting and waving at the boy from across the sand, but he just carried on, walking further into the water. In a blusterous fit, the man marched down the beach, grabbed the boy's arm and yanked him back to his mother, who was sunbathing and oblivious.

"Stupid little fucker," he said.

Elis watched as Gem's anxiety escalated, and started shoving stuff into a beach bag, suggesting they move to a different part of the beach. There would be no more haphazard counselling, and Gem vowed to revert to regular sessions, to delve further into such abnormal reactions.

*

The couple spent the final evening at the cinema, clutching a bucket of popcorn and sitting in coats as the heating was knackered. The vintage interior was a little musty, with old seating and red velvet curtains framing a big screen, and the usual nagging irritation of some punter's head obscuring the view.

"That bloke should take his hat off," Elis said, pointing.

The panama-hatted silhouette was reminiscent of the white-suited man, and just as the thought occurred, he did a full one-eighty.

"I think he heard you," Gem said.

There was no way he could be sitting right there, miles from the Clipper Café – if so, it was borderline creepy to think that he had followed them.

*

The thought of heading back home was deflating, and Gem was taking her sweet time packing bags and preparing to face life once again. Hiding away wasn't the answer, and sooner or later the retreat would become a trudge, a linear existence with no light and shade. Elis was the exact opposite, an avoider of overthinking and ready to jump the next hurdle, no matter how challenging.

The van was loaded, and Elis was waiting behind the wheel, staring through the passenger window. Gem was still inside, taking one last look around before rounding off her first holiday-home experience. She stepped out and nearly choked at the sight of a jet-black spider, spanning the small glass window set within the cottage door. This, it would seem, was the way of it now – larger-than-life arachnids at every turn, the reason for which was as clear as mud.

*

Monday showed, far too soon, as did the prospect of explaining away Gem's impromptu 'sickness', but Adrian didn't ask any questions and seemed otherwise distracted, as if he had far more important things on his mind.

Chapter 9

A night out to celebrate Jenny's new ownership of the café was looming, and Gem was getting ready to wear the dress she had bought especially for the occasion. It was worthy, given the steady progress of Clipper since moving into the flat, which had been a true saviour.

Gem made her way to the tube station, psychologically checking the contents of her bag – plasters to appease annoying shoe chafes, tissues, making sure there enough charge on her phone to call for a taxi, etc. She quickened her pace in the flimsiest of shoes and almost stumbled as the white-suited man appeared from behind a bus shelter.

"Hello, my dear," he said, tipping his panama hat.

Rache was right about the voice: a dark, velvety lilt of a proper English gentleman.

While busy thinking of excuses to escape, he reached into his coat pocket and took out a black gemstone in a gilt casing, hanging on a silver chain.

"I understand you have a score to settle," he said, staring deep into her eyes.

The intrusive, but very poignant, question left her in no doubt that he could indeed read her mind.

"If you say so," she said.

"Take this," he said, handing her the pendant. "When you are absolutely sure – and remember, there is no going back – press the sapphire."

"And then what?" she said.

"You'll see – take good care now," he said.

Gem watched as he continued down the street and then just filtered into the pavement.

Gem stood for a while, trying to mentally digest the strangest of encounters. The gemstone was heavy and ice-cold, it's dusty black surface hypnotic and calming, just as she had felt previously when the man was nearby. Suddenly, she was intrinsically drawn to the inanimate object, its allure filling her head with twisted and vengeful thoughts of tearing at her mother's flesh with bare hands. In a head shake, she threw the necklace in her bag and continued on as before. It surely couldn't be genuine, even though everything tied in.

*

The gang's wine-induced smiles shone out from across the bar as Rache, Jenny and two other new staff members gathered around a table. So much for being the first one there, Gem thought. It was a subtle reminder of when she met Polly for drinks during the first weeks of college and how things had significantly changed and for countless reasons. Gem ordered a large glass of red wine and promptly slugged it down to help with the shaking and dampen the weirdest of delusions.

"You needed that, right?" Rache said.

"Absolutely," Gem said.

As the evening progressed, multiple cross-routed conversations filtered through the Clipper crowd, while Gem sat back on her chair, replaying the intrinsic details of her liaison with the white-suited man. Whether justified or some sick hoax, it was an essential fantasy, fuelling an insatiable desire to get even, akin to stabbing a 'Hattie' voodoo doll with blunted pins.

*

Gem crept in at some unearthly hour, having walked part of the way home. The black gemstone had distanced her from reality, hence the repeated bag checks to make sure it was still there, further delaying the journey. Elis was asleep on the sofa, which was a godsend, given her boozy, irrational state, in a world where she had been set adrift on a splintered boat.

With the vaguest of light in the sky, Gem was staring up at the ceiling, lost in a blank-walled surface. She couldn't remember Elis coming to bed or even leaving for work, even though the covers were crumpled on his side. With nil intent, she threw on her dressing gown to go make some coffee and found her favourite cup suitably prepared on the worktop with the usual note: 'See you later, gorgeous'. Even a double caffeine hit couldn't mask the angst in a tunnel of torturous screams.

Gem made a conscious effort to get ready and found her bag on the carpet with its contents strewn, including the sapphire, its icy embrace stinging her skin on contact. The stench of death and dark shadows filled the room. Her open jaw exuded breathy growls while twisting a handful of skirt into a crumpled knot. Severed voices doused her ears: "What do we have here? A sister who robs you blind, a henpecked boyfriend who flips from squeaky clean to total jackass with one sniff of the Lesky slut, deceitful, backstabbing work colleagues, and the icing on the cake – *your mother*."

"Christ, I don't need this," she said, slinging the pendant down the toilet pan and flushing twice to make sure it had left the U-bend.

*

A hefty 'to-do' pile awaited as Gem rolled up late for work, relieved that Adrian was across the city, attending some business meeting. She looked down at her tea-stained shirt and remembered grabbing something from the pre-washing pile while dressing in a rush, her numb brain momentarily dissociating from real life.

Top of the list was a Cork and Hammond logo quote to promote a company merge, signed by Fran – the hierarchy delving into a hollow pit for creative assistance. Gem wished she could just rip it up into tiny pieces, but sibling disharmony shouldn't stand in the way of business, especially from such a high-flying organisation.

*

Angela's response to the voicemail finally came, and Gem dived into the ladies' toilet for complete privacy. She was much more mistrustful and suspicious of people, the spawn of many a deceitful being who had entered her life, and enhanced by the Pineapple Indigo staffroom eavesdrop.

"Sorry for not getting back sooner – I haven't been well," Angela said.

"That's okay – I felt bad for missing an appointment and wanted to arrange another," Gem said.

"As long as you are sure," Angela said.

Graham and Pat were on the sofa, glugging house red as Gem rolled in, feeling guilty for having forgotten about the dinner date.

"I won't be long," she said, heading straight for the bedroom to freshen up.

She peered into the mirror on passing, as one does when feeling out of sorts, not expecting to see the black sapphire pendant lying on the dresser. Maybe Elis had rescued it from the toilet bowl, its random reappearance awakening a strong sense of foreboding that the task to which she had been consigned wasn't for bargaining.

The conversation distinctly subsided as Gem entered the lounge, except for some distinct words concerning Joseph's welfare.

"We were just talking about Beth," Elis said, tripping over his tongue.

"Why, has something happened?" Gem said.

"Joseph's been missing school, and I'm worried that she's using again," he said.

"We've tried so hard with that girl," Pam said.

The shushy debate was a little mysterious, leaving Gem to consider, once again, what the fuck else was there left to discover about Elis's paternal history?

"Drug dependence is a rocky road, unfortunately," Gem said. "But Beth has a child – you should have told me, all of you."

Gem hated conceit and clumsy faux pas, so she left the lounge to gather her wits and refill her glass. Elis eventually opened up about Beth's heroin addiction, confiding that she had been in and out of rehab, which was the real reason why it had been difficult to arrange paternal visits. Graham and Pat had tried to support her during the pregnancy and the baby's first months, so they part-funded the rent for a nearby flat. Being alone with a screaming kid drew Beth like a magnet to a dealer who lived a few doors away, and the occasional recreational hit then became a serious habit. Life was a mixed bag of shit and silver, and Gem sure as hell didn't need yet another tortured tale bleeding into the room.

"I'm sure that between us we can pick up the pieces, but no more fucking secrets," Gem said.

*

Another sleepless interlude dragged Gem into the small hours, floating on some satanic wave and feasting on the one deed that would set things straight. By its very nature, she couldn't even imagine sharing such a bizarre quandary, least of all with Elis – who would completely flip, seeing it as some crazy monologue, and advise her to steer clear of blokes doling out weird jewellery. Regardless, only she could quantify the depth of hatred she felt for her mother and a wilful desire to exact her horrific demise.

Under normal circumstances, Gem would have been insanely late for work *again*, but today was an altogether different beast, in more ways than one. Nothing was going to change what had been devised; she must somehow calm the inner storm and face the prospect of returning to *that house*. Hattie was now the shit-smear and Gem was a holier-than-thou freaking arch-enemy, ready for battle.

The bathroom cabinet was packed with over-the-counter painkillers and Elis's medication, including Amitriptyline – a sedative he used to help him sleep. Gem had no concept of dosage and its subsequent effect, so took two tablets with several glugs of water.

Her reflection was morose, with pupils like black beads and the surrounding sclera peppered with veined streaks of red at each corner, enhanced by a ghostly pale complexion. This was a feeling no like no other, a rabid infestation of pure hatred.

Gem took the pendant from the dresser and placed it around her neck, focusing on the glistening gemstone and its undeniably hypnotic fusion. The connection between the white-suited man and the sapphire was now conclusive, though how and why were the unknowns. Revenge was Gem's only option.

The Amitriptyline's desensitising karma slowly kicked in, blurring her peripheral vision. She grabbed her bag and climbed into the taxi that was parked outside, trying to walk steadily as the fresh air intensified the drug's hallucinogenic stupor. The hour-long journey to Lanebridge magnified her senses – the sour aroma of sweat and pungent petrol fumes brought bitter, stinging tears, and the driver's every cough and sniff bellowed through the glass partition. He kept glancing back through the rear-view mirror, likely thinking she might vomit on the back seat.

They drove past the railway station and back towards the café where she first contemplated freedom, albeit in its many parts. Lanebridge village church was now derelict, its gates chained and cluttered with weed overgrowth and litter. The main street evoked memories of the impromptu meeting with Dan and the Lesky girl. Although an unfortunate slight, it was typical adolescent behaviour, if a little goddamn rude.

"Here's fine," she said, yards from the exact location.

*

The pathway to number seven Seaton Road, with its crooked garden gate, evoked queasy rumbles in Gem's gut. The swinging garden seat must have finally succumbed to Hattie's hefty frame as there were only rust marks on the decking where the rusty structure once stood.

A distinct smell of old chip fat and fustiness met Gem has she entered the lion's lair. There were dirty dishes piled high in the kitchen sink and general dilapidation, suggesting things had markedly worsened. Maybe Fran's theft had bled the old witch dry, or lifting just one finger was beyond her capability.

The sound of intrusion, and Gem's footsteps over the one squeaky floorboard, roused Hattie from her bed. She eventually opened the bedroom door and grunt-shuffled down the hall.

"Here she is," Gem said.

"What do you want?" Hattie said, with saliva-soaked jowls.

"I think even you can work that one out," Gem said, backing her mother towards the cellar door and watching as she stumbled and scratched her way down the stony steps.

Hattie lay crumpled and writhing in pain, mumbling some incoherent shit about Gem having abandoned a frail, helpless old woman.

"So, you were raped by one of Malc's employees and somehow that was my fault – is that why you were so goddamn cruel?"

"Ah, what would you know?"

"I was *still* your daughter, flesh and fucking blood."

"I look at you and all I see is that maniac thrusting into me."

"Then why didn't you go to the police instead of letting him walk free?"

A stare-out ensued, while Gem revelled at the prospect of severing the root of her misery.

"Let's start over," Hattie said, coughing and spluttering. "I could learn to love you."

"Yeah, you could switch right back and pretend Malc had never told you about the DNA test – I don't think so."

Gem stared down at the gibbering heap of rancid flesh and, with a cast-iron will, reached for the black sapphire.

"There's no reasoning with an empty vessel," she said, pressing the gemstone with both thumbs.

The atmosphere shifted, and a violent deathly chill embraced the already darkened room. Gem began to levitate, her arms and legs morphing into long, spindly wires, flexing forwards to cast silk-like threads until Hattie was frozen within a grey tangled cocoon of twisted fibres. As was nature's torturous game – whether to devour, or taunt like a cat clawing at an injured bird – Gem watched as the life slowly drained from her mother's body. In the final moment, the heart deflates like a punctured balloon and the brain's signals inflame, causing sudden fits of movement, until – *death*.

"For years, I was your fucking slave, but at least, *I know* when to call it quits," Gem said, poking a talon through the tensile mesh and into Hattie's chest wall.

It was evil in the purest form, to rid the world of those who are gratified by hurting others. It had to be so.

The light from the cellar door gradually filtered through, and Gem was back in her own skin. Hattie's body shrivelled into a hollow shell before disintegrating into a fine ash, floating into a cloud of expired dust. The black sapphire was nothing more than a lump of plastic hanging on a tacky chain, like the ones within split plastic globes in novelty-toy machines.

Yards from the dissipating carnage, Gem saw the old blanket that had been her only comfort on many an evening's consignment to the stone tomb. A bony hand was poking out from beneath and, on lifting it further, Gem discovered a fractured skeleton, randomly coated in shards of rotting flesh. It was the body of Mr Rake, who must have died after hitting his head on the kitchen floor then subsequently dragged into the cellar. There was never any doubt that Hattie would do *anything* in order to save herself, as she was the prime suspect of both Mr Rake and Gem's disappearance.

Raw justice had drawn the ugliest chapter of Gem's life to a close, but she couldn't leave without one last look inside her old bedroom. It was an empty shell, with nothing between the walls: no bed, no analogue television, no dilapidated dresser – and even the old carpet had been rolled up and propped in the corner. 'Lola', who once lived between the sofa cushions before Hattie's dysmorphia, was now perched on the windowsill with a flea-bitten face and one leg hanging, as if she had been pulled from the trash to mark the final insult.

"Hattie certainly got the better of you," she said, stroking Dollie's hand.

A loose stitch below her neckline had been torn into a visible hole, from which a jet-black spider emerged, crawling down the scaly paintwork towards the bare boards, a normal domestic spider with no unusual movement or crackle. Gem was of the belief that the previous spider sightings were illusions, just like the mood morphs, conducted by the white-suited man who came to save her, albeit in a very unique way.

The path to peace had been laid, and the first step was closing the door of *that house* for the final time: the ultimate cleansing.

There was someone in the neighbouring garden, concealed by the hedgerow. Mrs Oddly's daughter popped her head over to say hello, but Gem wasn't one for small talk and kept on walking.

"Good morning," she said. "Lovely day."

"Oh yes, it certainly is. How's your mum?" Gem said.

"She died a few weeks ago. I'm just getting the place ready for sale," she said.

"Sorry to hear that – she was lovely," Gem said.

"Thank you. Mothers – they're so precious, don't you think?"

*

The village supermarket was a familiar path, and Gem was curious to know whether Simone was still there, wearing invisible angel wings, and maybe in a new role as staff supervisor or assistant manager. The girl had been a true saviour, a veritable light in Gem's godforsaken life back then, and it would bring sheer joy just to say thank you for everything.

Sliding doors opened into the foyer, where villagers used to huddle together to share insults. Apart from periodic modifications, the layout was much the same: trollies to the left, shopping aisles straight ahead. Gem grabbed a basket so as to look inconspicuous, and headed to the customer service desk to make enquiries. A lady pointed her towards Lorraine, the head assistant, who stood over by the veggies.

"I've been here since the place opened, and we've never had a Simone working here – unless it was during the holidays, when we sometimes have helpers."

There was nothing to suggest that Simone had been a

temporary member of staff – she was always in full uniform, with a name tag and everything.

*

Elis had been the cook and general kitchen-dweller since moving in, and he deserved a wholesome two-course dinner with all the trimmings. Gem laid the table and waited, just like he did for her – every night, at whatever time. There was cause for celebration, but one that could never be shared – sinister and yet magical in its entirety – and with the perfect partner, a wonderful home and a job born of her own merits. What more could one possibly ask for?

There were many messages outstanding on the answerphone: Elis's manager, spouting about outstanding repairs; Adrian, querying her absence; and Fran, with a post-housewarming mammoth rant that sure as hell wasn't an apology: "Hi, sis, just wondered how you were – what do you say we meet for coffee?"

Was this a joke? Who was this woman, sounding like some imposter, reciting from the 'how to be nice' textbook?

Elis finally arrived home, seduced by food aromas that were not of his own creation.

"Wow, have I missed an important date?" he said, being a teensy bit sarcastic.

"No, I just felt it was about time I did some cooking," Gem said.

Elis's perception was insurmountable. Once again, sensing that something was a little different to previously, and he was right. The pervasive unparalleled sadness that had held her in a vice-like grip forever was now gone.

"You just seem so, so …"

"Changed?" she said.

*

The phone kept on ringing throughout dinner, as though whoever it was didn't know when to quit, forcing Elis to slam down the cutlery and answer the damned call.

"If it's for me, I'm not here," Gem said, stuffing in another mouthful.

"It's Fran," Elis said, holding out the handset.

"I'll ring her back later," she said.

Elis sat back down, wearing a disparaging look, like Gem was purposely ignoring her hellish sister. As if.

"I know she's a pain, but you really should give her another chance," he said.

"Well, she walked out of here, remember?"

"I get it, but there was something about her voice, you know – she sounded different."

*

Gem went for a walk in the park and stopped for coffee at the stall where Phil was last seen mauling one of his floozies, or so it appeared. It was the first clear day, free of past evils, consigned to the 'fuck it' drawer of nil debate or deconstruction. She took the steepest route, and kept climbing though trees and out the other side, remembering nature and its unique cleansing. The therapy had been journey of self-realisation, and how best to move on without past shackles, such was the bitter irony. Angela's wisdom would always remain, like an embracing robe of clichés:

Imagine you are looking out so far into the distance that the line between land and sky can only be defined by your own interpretation, as is your future.

The mental note to call Fran had followed Gem back home, and she stared at the phone for several minutes prior to dialling the number, wishing it would just ring out and save her soul from yet another sour conversation.

"Hi, sis, how are you?" Fran said.

"Yes, I'm good," Gem said.

"Thanks for getting back – so, would you like to meet up?"

Gem thought for a moment. It just didn't add up, unless, by some miracle, the woman had had a personality reset or turned to religion or some such. Maybe she was just making a conscious effort to build bridges – and everyone deserves a second chance, right? To keep things simple, Gem thought of the obvious place; at least it was neutral ground, should all go south.

"What about the Clipper Café, around midday?"

"Absolutely – see you there, later."

*

Gem took a bus to the chosen meeting place, a very short journey where there simply wasn't time to gather the strength to fight back should Fran be faking it. At least the café was genuinely different, all spruced up with modern tables and chairs indoors and out, sheltered beneath a striped awning. Gem had been expecting to wait around but could see Fran by the window, where the white-suited man used to sit. Rache was at the counter, looking equally surprised to see the sober sister.

"The order's already in," she said.

Gem walked over and sat down, placing her bag on the chair.

"So, how's it going?" she said.

"All good, it's so lovely to see you," Fran said.

There was, indeed, a sweet and wholesome young lady sitting before her – with no pretences such as hair dye, false eyelashes or stealth lipstick – looking rather sedate in a regular patterned shirt and jeans.

"You've certainly changed since the housewarming," Gem said.

"Yes, sorry for leaving early. I wasn't feeling too good."

Gem didn't have the heart to challenge someone for whom butter seemingly wouldn't melt – and anyway, she was so done with conflict.

Rache brought two cups of coffee and lemon drizzle cake over to the table, glancing over her shoulder as she walked back to the counter.

"How did you know I liked cappuccino with chocolate sprinkles?" Gem said.

"You told me," Fran said.

Gem was slowly softening to the depiction of everyone's favourite sibling, of the sisterly connection she had sorely craved.

"I got your quote for the logo," Gem said,

"That's great – I met Adrian at a recent training event and he told me all about you."

They proceeded to talk business and about life in general, with not a single mention of past traumas, as if that mental slate had been wiped clean.

"So where do you live now?"

"Beedon Court. Don't you remember?"

Was this the snagging point, Gem thought, having left the flat because she believed it was about to be repossessed?

"Yes, I just thought the landlord …"

"He was always confusing me with the neighbour who never paid the rent."

A couple of young guys stood outside the café, smoking dodgy ciggies, and it wasn't long before the obnoxious fumes filtered in through the open window.

"Jeez, would you get a whiff of ganja?" Gem said, subtly poking the nest.

"I know – makes me gag," Fran said.

"You, erm, never tried it then?" Gem said, peering above the rim of her coffee cup.

"Do I look like the sort who would?"

"No, actually, you don't."

The black sapphire had claimed both Hattie *and* the associated psychological carnage inflicted on her children. It was if *she* had never graced the earth, thanks to the white-suited man – the devil's advocate.

Cruelty is a moral judgment, implying the ability to reflect upon the meaning and consequences of one's behaviour.

About the Author

I am a true 'Yorkshire lass', as they say, born and bred in Sheffield, where I have always lived.

My love of reading was present from childhood, and in particular, limericks. During my teenage years, my favourite authors were Fay Weldon and Martin Amis.

In 2012, I wrote 'An Ordinary Life', a biographical story, written in the third person, using fictional characters. What began as a therapeutic exercise and with no expectation as to where it would lead, the title was finally published.

My literary journey continued with The Healing, inspired by my passion for the paranormal, written to stoke speculative curiosity and for readers who share a particular interest in the dark side.

I have now completed my third novel, Black Sheep, which details the life of a little girl who exists within a fractured and abusive childhood and who finally escapes her cruel existence.

As an established author, I take great pleasure in the literary world where the stories just keep on flowing, and I am now penning outlines for my third and fourth titles.

E: smith.k51@sky.com
W: http://www.karenestokes.com
Facebook author page:
https://www.facebook.com/KEStokes.author

.

www.blossomspringpublishing.com

www.ingramcontent.com/pod-product-compliance
Lightning Source LLC
Chambersburg PA
CBHW020436180626
46812CB00003B/1256